THE
WOMAN
IN OUR
MARRIAGE

BOOKS BY VICTORIA JENKINS

The Divorce

The Argument

The Accusation

The Playdate

The New Family

The Bridesmaids

The Midwife

Happily Married

Your Perfect Life

The Open Marriage

The Mother's Phone Call

DETECTIVES KING AND LANE SERIES

The Girls in the Water

The First One to Die

Nobody's Child

A Promise to the Dead

THE WOMAN IN OUR MARRIAGE

VICTORIA JENKINS

bookouture

Published by Bookouture in 2025

An imprint of Storyfire Ltd.
Carmelite House
50 Victoria Embankment
London EC4Y 0DZ

www.bookouture.com

The authorised representative in the EEA is Hachette Ireland
8 Castlecourt Centre
Dublin 15 D15 XTP3
Ireland
(email: info@hbgi.ie)

ISBN: 978-1-83618-058-6
eBook ISBN: 978-1-83618-057-9

For Antonia Collett, my beta reader, and for Melinda Stefan, who inspired the beautiful accent

PROLOGUE

'Let me take him,' I say, trying to keep the words from wobbling with the fear that's rising in my gut.

'I don't think that's a good idea.'

The words cut through the air between us.

'You're not coping. You know that, deep down.'

It's then that I notice the glass on the bedside table, half filled with water. Or half empty? I look again at my son, curled on the bed, sleeping too soundly, without a care in the world. Our arguing should have woken him. He's slept right through it.

'What have you given him?'

'Just something to let him sleep.'

'He's just a child,' I say, my voice cracking as I fight to maintain a pretence of calm.

'He'll be fine. It's just to give you some space and time. That's all you've ever really needed.'

'What I need,' I say, gritting my teeth, 'is the truth. That's all I've ever really needed.'

'And you know you'll always get that from me.'

But it's a lie. All of it is lies.

When I make a lunge for Noah, I'm grabbed by the arm and

yanked back sharply. A hand moves deftly to a pocket, pulling out a syringe.

'There's enough in here to make sure he never wakes again. I don't want to do it so please don't make me. But I promise you, if you try to take him from this room, I'll do it. And there'll be no going back from it.'

'Please,' I beg through tears. 'He's just a child. None of this has anything to do with him.'

'Then you need to do everything exactly as I tell you, and he won't get hurt.'

The bedside table is opened, and a writing pad and pen are taken out and handed to me.

'Your suicide note,' I'm told. 'Write it.'

PART ONE

SUZANNA

ONE

FRIDAY

The scream lasts longer than seems humanly possible. It is shrill and desperate, a torture klaxon. It pierces the night, ricocheting off every corner in the darkness. It's the cry of a woman: anguished, traumatised... the kind of scream that precedes a deathly silence. This woman's pain seems to stretch beyond the bounds of what a person can be expected to endure. I try to shut myself off from the noise of it, from the agony that surfs on the crest of its pitch.

And then I realise the scream belongs to me.

There are hands on my shoulders, shaking me from sleep. Matthew's voice desperately speaks my name, slicing through the scream and cutting it dead.

'Suzanna.'

My eyes remain shut tight, my brain still trapped in sleep. Still trapped within the nightmare I know will continue once my eyes are opened.

'Suzanna. You're okay. It was just a dream.'

The room is sunk in darkness other than for the light seeping in beneath the bottom of the bedroom door. We always leave the bathroom light on for Noah, in case he wakes in the night and wanders into our room. It's been nearly a year since he last did that, but we repeat this nightly tradition anyway, ever expectant. Ever hopeful.

My pyjamas feel damp with sweat as I stir into wakefulness. But the image from the nightmare doesn't leave when I open my eyes. Instead, it sits at the front of my mind, reminding me that there is no escape from it.

'Do you want to talk about it?' Matthew asks.

'No. I'm okay.'

This happens every few nights now, the same nightmare returning to haunt me. I can't talk about it – not with Matthew, at least. I can barely bring myself to recall its details: the sights and sounds of it; the taste of fear it leaves sitting on my tongue even long after its reel has played out.

Matthew runs a hand over my bare arm as he returns to the bed to lie beside me. He's already dressed and ready for work, probably due to leave. He's out of the house by 5.30 a.m. five mornings a week; the gyms he owns all open early, and he likes to be an active part of the running of them. Though when he is home, he may as well not be. He might say the right words at the right time, but I know he can barely stand to be in the same room as me any more.

'Are you going to be okay? Reka's awake... I heard her up and about earlier. She can get Noah ready for nursery later. Did you remember to take your meds yesterday?'

I'm currently taking a cocktail of sleeping remedies and mood enhancers, but I know he's referring to the Zoloft Jess prescribed for my PTSD. Since I started therapy with her, she's trialled several different medications to try to help with my anxiety and erratic sleep patterns. Sometimes I forget to take them. On my worst days, it's all I can manage to do to get dressed.

'Yes,' I tell him. 'I remembered.'

Concern etches his forehead. He expected them to have

more of an effect by now. Perhaps I did too, yet the nightmares are managing to get worse – more vivid, more frequent. Perhaps we are both trying to fool ourselves by believing for a moment that something as simple as a pill will make our heartbreak go away. For as long as I breathe, it is here. It can never be erased.

'When are you next seeing Jess?'

'Monday.'

Matthew lingers for a moment, poised to say something more, but whatever it is gets swallowed when he tells me he'd better go and check on Noah. He gets up and leaves the room to go and see to our four-year-old son, who I've no doubt woken prematurely again with my nightmares. Matthew leaves the door ajar, and I hear him speaking our son's name, softly trying to coax a response that is unlikely to be offered. Noah barely speaks any more. Not to me, at least. Occasionally I will hear him talk to Reka, a few incoherent words mumbled on his half-breath. The sound of these alone is enough to rip a hole in my heart. He can talk to this young woman who has been with us for a little over four months – this woman who is still in so many ways a stranger – but he can't bring himself to speak to me.

Because we know too much of each other now. Already, though he is barely beyond his toddler years.

I hear Reka's voice float along the landing, the gentle inflections of her accented speech drifting through the bedroom door.

'Is everything okay?' she asks. And then I hear my name, but I don't catch what comes after it.

When Matthew responds, he keeps his voice lowered. I wonder whether it's to keep his words from being overheard by Noah or by me. I get out of bed quietly and slip to the bedroom door. When I peer out, I see Matthew standing outside Reka's bedroom, his hand pressed to the door frame. His shirt is loose at his waist, not tucked in tidily. Even from the side, I can see how tired his face looks. Like me, he hasn't slept an uninterrupted night for almost a year now. But if he dreams, he never shares the details with me.

I can't see Reka. She's inside her room, talking to him from the privacy of her own space. We gave her the second bedroom with the en suite, so that she would have her privacy away from the family bathroom used by the rest of us. Her bedroom overlooks the wide expanse of garden at the back of the house. When she moved in, I told her she could decorate it how she liked. A year ago, I might have baulked at the idea of a stranger coming into our home and adapting it to suit their own tastes. Now, I don't care what she does with the place.

But you do care what she does with your husband.

The words reach my ears with a voice that's not my own. I turn against the bedroom wall, lean back, close my eyes and press my fingertips to my eyelids. The voices keep coming. They started a little while ago, usually arriving on the brink of sleep. My eyes will finally be dragged shut, my mind exhausted to the point of not being able to withstand the fight against it any longer, and then I will hear it.

You could be capable of even worse, you know.

You shouldn't still be breathing.

Suzanna, this is all your fault.

I can put my hands over my ears, squeeze my eyes shut so tightly it feels as though I might pass out; I can sprint through the lanes that surround our home until my lungs are heaved raw and my heart might burst. Nothing makes it stop. This is my life now.

When I look back along the landing, Reka has shifted from her room and is within sight. She is wearing pyjama shorts and a vest top despite the milder temperatures of spring having not yet reached us. Her bare leg is arched towards Matthew in an Angelina Jolie red carpet stance, smooth skin glistening beneath the light that pours from the bathroom.

You're being paranoid, I tell myself. *She's just standing in a doorway.*

But as I watch them, doubt trickles through my veins, making my skin tingle. And it's not the first time I've felt this. There's something about the way he leans against the door frame, his body tipped towards her. The way she looks at him so intently as he speaks. What are they still talking about? Why is Matthew still here?

And then he moves, turning to go to Noah's bedroom. I pull back into my own room sharply, not wanting Reka to catch a glimpse of me spying on them. I know I'm being ridiculous.

But what if you're not?

I go to the bed and pull up the duvet, airing it before laying it back on the mattress and smoothing it flat. I plump my pillows first before doing the same on Matthew's side of the bed. I once read somewhere that making your bed in the morning is a sign of starting your day off on the right foot, though it's never made much sense to me. I feel barely capable of making it downstairs, of simply putting one foot in front of the other to function. A smoothed-out duvet isn't going to change anything.

Something makes me stop as I'm returning Matthew's top pillow to the bed. Across the pale pink and lemon-yellow patterned cotton, there's a hair. A long hair. I lift it carefully from the pillowcase between my thumb and forefinger, holding it up to the light. The hair is too long to be mine. It is too light in colour. Blonde. I sit on Matthew's side of the bed and drape the single strand across my palm. Through the open door and from down the landing, I hear the low hum of music coming from her room as she begins to get ready for the day. She is singing along quietly, her muted tones drifting to the staircase. She has forgotten my torment already, oblivious to events on the other side of her door.

I study the hair again for a moment before picking it up. She's been here. With him. Reka and Matthew, here together.

TWO

FRIDAY

I'm not sure how I spend the morning. At some point I manage to fold some of Noah's clothes and return them to the wardrobe in his bedroom, and I eat a piece of toast in the garden, still wearing my dressing gown. I heard the car pull off the gravel driveway when Reka went to collect Noah from nursery, but other than these small details, my mind seems completely blank.

In the garden of this detached Georgian property that Matthew inherited from an aunt who'd had no children, I could be sitting anywhere. Maidstone is just a short drive away, but with the front of the house protected from a tall hedgerow that cuts it off from view of the lane beyond, and with the wide expanse of garden that drops down to the river and the woodland behind, I am a world away from the rest of civilisation, alone with just the morning air and my thoughts. This peace and isolation was something we chose, with the belief that it might offer us a simpler, calmer life. Now, I feel like a prisoner here, incarcerated by the history held between those four walls.

At just before 1.30 p.m., I am back inside the house, upstairs in the bedroom. I hear something being dropped in the kitchen. Noah will have had his lunch by now; Reka collected him from nursery two hours ago, and their usual routine when the weather is dry is to come home, read stories together in the kitchen while lunch is cooking, eat together and then play in the garden until I take over at four o'clock. Sometimes, on the days I feel able to leave the house, I'll go to collect Noah myself. I bring him home, make him lunch... move through the motions of existing. Reka fills the spaces I leave void, the understudy for a role I can no longer perform.

Another crash comes from downstairs. My nerves in tatters, I get up off the bed, where I've lain inert for the past hour, unable to summon the energy to complete any of the tasks that require my attention: the wet washing that still sits in the machine, the admin I've been ignoring for weeks, the freshly dug flower bed that I turned over a couple of weeks ago and then abandoned. I feel dizzy just standing, my head light from all the joy that's been stolen from my heart. Sick with exhaustion and fear and grief.

When I get to the kitchen, Reka is at the sink. A stack of pans towers by the draining board, ready to be returned to the cupboard.

'Sorry,' she says, when she sees me come in. 'Did I disturb you? I'm so clumsy.'

'You're fine.'

'I was going to make a coffee,' she says, gesturing to the machine. 'Would you like one?'

I shake my head, declining the offer. Caffeine is probably the last thing I need. My nerves are already jangling. I feel like I might be sick.

'Suzanna,' Reka says. She reaches for a tea towel and dries her hands before adjusting the floral headband she always wears. 'Are you okay? You look like the sheet.'

I manage a laugh. These little confusions in Reka's English have always been endearing, and sometimes they've managed to raise smiles between Matthew and me – a brief respite from the misery that has hung between us over this past year. She told me when she first came to the house that she'd only started learning English a few years earlier. I wondered at the time whether she'd hoped to partake in more conversation once she moved here, that being immersed in the language day-to-day would help develop her ability, but she'd known before that first visit what she was letting herself into by coming to us.

'I look white as a sheet,' I say. 'Is that what you mean? Or just that I look like shit? I won't be offended by either.'

I give her a smile so that she knows I'm only teasing and not trying to mock her, but her cheeks pinken and I feel bad for embarrassing her.

'White like the sheet,' she assures me. 'Are you sure you're okay?'

I remember the way I saw her with Matthew this morning, the exchange between them at her bedroom door. My guilt at having embarrassed her slips from me.

'I'm fine.'

I look at the dining table, where Noah's stories and an opened colouring book are stacked. 'Where's Noah?'

Reka's eyes narrow. 'I don't know... He's been with you, Suzanna.'

I feel a pain in my chest, a tightening around my heart. 'What do you mean? He's with you... You picked him up.'

'Yes, and then you came to me and told me you wanted to spend time with him this afternoon, that I wouldn't be needed.' Her voice has a defensive edge, her words sharp and clipped. 'I see you just now,' she adds, 'and I think he might be taking a nap.'

'Reka,' I say, trying to stay calm, 'there's some misunderstanding. I haven't seen you since this morning, before you took Noah to nursery.'

She looks at me as though I've just slapped her across the

face. 'You came to me, Suzanna,' she tells me again. She folds her arms across her chest. 'So where is he?'

It feels as though she's testing me. Why would she do this? Why would she taunt me in such a cruel way?

'Where's my son, Reka?'

'I don't know, Suzanna,' she says again, slowing her words as though she's talking to a child. 'He was with you.'

I turn and leave the kitchen, going through to the living room, where I half expect to find Noah curled up on the sofa watching television. He has far too much screen time these days – more than I'd ever planned to allow. When he was a baby, I had a fixed idea on how Matthew and I would raise our child. We would spend most of our time outdoors, regardless of the weather; he would be an explorer, raised on homemade meals for which we'd grown the ingredients together in our picture-perfect vegetable garden; he'd be encouraged to ask questions and be curious about the world around him. Now, I scrape myself from bed in the mornings just to offer him the basic care of food and clothing. He can't even speak to me, and I wonder sometimes if he's scared of me. I find excuses not to be around him. We are barely able to look one another in the eye. I know he deserves so much better.

'Noah!'

I look behind the sofa and the floor-length curtains that hang at the living room's bay window, but Noah is not here. I head from there into the conservatory, which for the past year has been used for little more than hanging out washing and housing piles of folded laundry. Other than for this, the place is empty. Noah isn't here.

Panic begins to rise in my chest. What if one of the doors has been left open? From our garden, it's easy enough to access the rest of the land we inherited along with the house. Some of it is so overgrown it's barely accessible. Noah is small, and if he was to get lost in the woodland, he would never be able to find his way back to the house. We'd planned to fence off the garden so that it was safe for him to roam without constant supervision, but we never got around to it.

From the conservatory doors, which are never opened, I look out on to the expanse of lawn. The climbing frame near the ancient oak tree is empty, its swing hanging perfectly still. If Noah has been in the garden today, he hasn't been near his favourite spot – not recently, at least.

'Noah!'

I call for him again as I turn back and head for the hallway. When I get there, I see Reka at the top of the stairs.

'He's not in his bedroom.'

I rush into the kitchen and go through the patio doors to the garden. They've been left unlocked. Noah's football is resting next to the sand tray that hasn't been used since the summer, and his balance bike lies abandoned by the shed.

'Noah!' I head across the lawn, past the flower beds where my spade still lies in the turned-over soil. 'Noah!' I run past the summer house, down to the bottom of the garden and across the makeshift bridge that passes over the tiny stream that runs through our land. Shallow water.

But enough for a small child to drown in.

I hear footsteps behind me. Reka.

'He won't have come down here. He knows not to go this far.'

Her words grate on my nerves. I know she's only trying to help, but she talks sometimes as though she knows my child better than I do.

Perhaps she does.

'And he always listens, does he?' I respond sharply.

She says nothing. She understands. Noah may have listened up until today, but there's a first time for everything.

I stare past the gate that lies a few metres ahead and look across the expanse of fields and woodland that stretches beyond, acres and acres of it, most of it barely yet trodden by our feet since we moved here. There are makeshift paths, but some have steep drops down and he could so easily slip. There's the stream, which leads to the river, where the boundary of our land meets with that of a neighbouring farm. It will get dark in just a few hours' time...

'I'm calling the police.'

'Suzanna—'

Reka follows me as I hurry back to the house. I have no idea where I left my phone, and we can't waste time: the more minutes that pass, the more time Noah has in which to get further away. I go into the kitchen and scan the surfaces for my mobile phone.

'Suzanna, is this necessary? Noah must surely be here somewhere.'

Ignoring Reka, I go into the hallway and head up to my bedroom. I can't remember whether I had the phone up there with me earlier, but I assume I must have; perhaps it's slipped on to the carpet or I've left it on the bedside table. I don't make it as far as the bedroom when I hear a noise coming from along the landing. Crying. It's coming from the nursery.

I stop outside the bathroom door and close my eyes, steadying myself with a hand pressed to the door frame when I hear the sound grow louder. I try to breathe in the way I've been taught – in for four seconds and slowly out for eight – but my heart continues to pound in my chest and my palms feel slippery with sweat. I squeeze my eyes shut tighter, but the sound of the crying continues.

I no longer know whose cries I'm hearing, whether they're hers or Noah's. All I know is I cannot let anything happen to my son.

THREE

FRIDAY

For a moment, there was nothing. I could see nothing. I could hear nothing. I felt nothing. When I eventually come around, I'm not sure how long I've been standing here, with my palm pressed to the bathroom door frame and my head lowered, the blood rushing to my brain. It's like a switch is flicked and I'm back on the landing. The first thing I hear is Reka calling Noah's name. Then I remember... we were looking for him.

When I open my eyes, I see a flash of a green sweater in my peripheral vision. Reka.

I turn to see her at the door of the nursery, and my heart jolts in my chest. No one ever goes in that room. She shouldn't be going into that room.

'Reka!'

I race after her, rushing through the nursery doorway in a flood of panic. Once there, I barely notice her. All I see is the room, untouched since that day: the crocheted blanket hanging from the armchair near the window, the soft toys lined up on the chest of drawers, the picture that hangs in a frame above the cot – name, date and weight embroidered in tiny detail beneath a patchwork hot air balloon.

'Please leave,' I say quietly, barely able to utter the words. She shouldn't be putting me in this position. She knows not to come in here. No one comes in here.

'Suzanna—'

'We have no rules here,' I remind her. 'No rules except this one.'

She puts a hand on my arm, her fingertips gripping me too tightly. I go to shake her off, but then I realise she's trying to communicate something to me.

From the corner of my eye, I see something move in the cot. The patterned bumper that lines the wooden slats is blocking the view, but at the foot of the cot, the quilt shifts. Through a blur of silent tears, my vision wobbles. I am somewhere else: the same room, but a different time. She has been crying again, restless and unsettled, fractious anywhere other than in my arms. The room is steeped in darkness, just a shard of yellow light slicing through the opened doorway from the landing. Her cries are staccato, stop-start, stop-start, a metronome with each beat louder than the last. I lift her from the mattress and hold her close to my chest, rocking from side to side to try to soothe her, knowing that it won't work, because nothing seems to calm her. I can smell the baby shampoo I washed her hair with earlier. I can hear her staggered cries as she tries to catch her breath.

'Suzanna. He needs you.'

Everything shifts as Reka's words snap me back to the present. The movement in the cot changes; a leg is drawn up as its owner curls in on himself. Noah. He is here, balled into a foetal position in his sister's cot. He never comes in here. We've never had to tell him not to, because he's never shown any interest in doing so. If anything, he has avoided her bedroom, never venturing along the landing further than the bathroom. I'd assumed it was an act of subconscious self-preservation, that by staying away from the nursery Noah was protecting himself from the new reality of what our lives have become. But when I see him now, his little features frozen in fear, I wonder whether we've done the right thing in encouraging him to avoid all memory of her. Perhaps we've inadvertently made everything worse.

Reka's hand returns to my arm, and her touch sends a wave of resentment rushing through me. She is trying to prompt me, trying to push me to do something I'm not capable of doing. What am I supposed to say to my son? That it's all okay? That everything will be all right? It's not, and it won't be.

'Noah,' Reka says gently, 'it's okay.'

She moves tentatively towards the cot, her movements cautious because of me, not him. She is waiting for me to react, for me to stop her. I know she's doing what I should be doing, yet my brain keeps my body rooted to the spot, not allowing me to move to get closer to him.

I can feel my heart racing, my skin slick with sweat beneath my pyjama top. Why is he here, in her room? What is he doing lying in her cot? A knot forms in my stomach. I try to push it down, but it rises to my chest, my throat, my mouth. I can taste it on my tongue, thick and sour and suffocating.

'Get out of there,' I say quietly.

Reka turns to look at me, wide-eyed. 'Suzanna.'

'Get out of there!'

She moves to the cot, puts a hand inside to run a reassuring palm over Noah's back. 'Suzanna, please, you're scaring him.'

And then Noah starts sobbing. I know I should go to him, but I can't. I should apologise... I should hold him... I should do something. All I can hear are Annabelle's cries.

Reka reaches for Noah and lifts him out of the cot. He clings to her like a koala, and she avoids eye contact with me as she carries him from the room. I hear them go down the landing to his bedroom; she soothes him with words, but I can't make out what she says. All I can hear is Annabelle, her shrill, desperate cries piercing my ears.

I don't know how long I stay here in her room. Time seems to have stopped again because the next thing I'm aware of is Reka putting a hand on my arm, helping me up from the floor.

'Come on,' she says. 'I made you a tea.'

'Where's Noah?'

'He fell asleep. I put him in his bed.'

I follow her along the landing like a zombie, down the stairs and into the hallway. 'Go and sit down,' she instructs me, gesturing to the living room. 'I will bring the tea for you.'

I do as she says and go into the living room, but when she hasn't reappeared a minute or two later, I go down the hallway to the kitchen, where I hear Reka's voice, lowered to hushed tones.

'I don't know,' I hear her say. 'Like she froze, I guess.'

I peer into the kitchen but cannot see her, before realising that she's crouched in the utility room, trying to keep herself hidden from sight. A shadow falls before the door, across the small space that was years ago probably used as a larder. She falls silent while she waits for a response from the person at the other end of the call. Matthew. I picture him at work, taking her call from a changing room, having chosen to stay on at one of the gyms rather than have to face coming home to what is left of his family.

I think of that hair on our bed, and a vision pops into my mind: Reka's naked limbs sprawled on top of the duvet.

When she next speaks, her voice is lowered to little more than a whisper. I don't hear everything, but I hear enough. 'Not coping... needs proper help... getting worse.' And then she says something that sends a chill snaking through my veins, cooling my blood. 'Noah was scared of her.'

I can't listen to her any more. I go back to the living room, where I sit on the sofa with my head in my hands. Just a minute or so later, Reka appears in the doorway holding a cup of tea.

She puts it on a coaster on the coffee table and lingers at the side of the sofa, hesitant as she chooses her words.

'Can I get you something to eat? When did you last have something?'

But I barely hear her. Was my son really scared of me? The thought won't slip from my consciousness. He looked frightened, but I hadn't for a moment thought that it was me he feared. I'd assumed it was the room that had provoked the response – the enormity of being immersed in the memory of Annabelle. Perhaps I am so much worse than a negligent mother. Maybe Noah sees me as a monster.

'Suzanna?'

'I'm okay.'

'If you want to go to bed, I'll see to Noah when he wakes up. I can make him dinner.'

With my eyes squeezed tight, I can see Reka with Matthew. He is smiling, laughing at something she's just said. Noah is with them. Talking. Happy.

'No,' I say. 'I won't do that.'

Because she won't do this to me. I won't allow her to take my baby.

FOUR

SATURDAY

I barely sleep on Friday night, so I spend much of Saturday in a stupor, not knowing what time of day it is. My only sense of time now comes during the week, when the days are structured around Noah going to nursery and coming home. The weekends pass in a fog of survival, just trying to make it from one day to the next. This Saturday is a particularly bad one. I fall asleep at some time during mid-morning and wake to a quiet bedroom. Noah must be with Matthew, where he is no doubt safer.

When I eventually go downstairs, the house is even more silent than usual. I peer into each room in turn, but Matthew and Noah are nowhere to be seen. Neither is Reka. I go into the kitchen and make myself a coffee, and when I go to the fridge to take out milk, the calendar on the wall reminds me that Matthew is attending a charity gala this evening. After returning to work following bereavement leave, Matthew threw himself into his job with greater ferocity than ever. He organised a winter fitness challenge that went viral and ended up raising over sixty thousand pounds for a local charity that supports terminally ill children and their families. The charity's director organised tonight's gala as a celebration of the event and a bid to push the total even higher.

Matthew asked me weeks ago if I wanted to join him, but I declined the invitation. Too many sympathetic smiles and awkward exchanges, because people still don't know what to say to us. They don't know what to say to me, at least. Over the winter, Matthew became something of a local celebrity, the media picking up on our tragic tale and his determination to build something positive from our loss. Inevitably, the circumstances of Annabelle's death became public knowledge. Sympathies fell upon Matthew. But for me it was very different. I didn't need to see much of what was written online to know that I was held accountable. The support he received for his charitable endeavours was an emotional crutch to Matthew, with the focus the project required of him offering a way to help navigate a path through his grief. But the more involved he became with work, the more I felt him slip away.

When I take my coffee into the living room, I pass by the front door. Reka's running trainers aren't on the shoe rack where they're usually placed, so I assume that she's gone out. I check my phone and there's a message from Matthew.

Taken Noah to soft play.

There's no kiss at the end of the text. No casual question over how I am, because he already knows the answer to that. I am always the same; nothing changes.

With everyone out of the house, I don't know what to do with myself. But I feel a need to do something. Anything. So, I pull the washing machine away from the wall in the utility room and move the vacuum cleaner and the ironing board into the kitchen. Out in one of the sheds, I find a tin of paint left over from when we first moved into the house, when a burst of energy and enthusiasm had us believing that we'd completely revamp and modernise the place within a month. Over that next year, we were going to renovate the outhouses as holiday rental properties. It was an ambitious plan, but with Matthew's energy and my creative vision, it was doable. It might have made us stronger, and I wonder if there remains a chance it could still do the same.

With the radio up loud and in a pair of old leggings and a T-shirt that was accidentally bleached in the wash, I start to cut in around the ceiling, not bothering to use masking tape to create a straighter line. The paint is watery and runs down the plaster in messy streaks. Perhaps the consistency has been altered by being left outside in the cold for so many years, but whatever – I keep going.

I don't hear the front door, so I almost fall off the dining chair I'm standing on when Jess appears in the utility room doorway, her hair and jacket wet with rain. Sometimes when I see her, I'm struck by how little she's changed in the two decades I've known her. She remains the girl I met at university, young and carefree and full of ideas.

'I'm sorry. I did ring the bell.' She needs to raise her voice to be heard above the music, and I hurriedly get down off the chair, go into the kitchen and turn the radio down.

'Is everything okay?' she asks.

This is how things are now – if I languish in bed all morning, I'm depressed; if I decide to do a spot of impromptu decorating, I'm in the grip of some kind of mania.

'I'm not sure,' I tell her. 'What do you think, does it look streaky?'

She plays along with my attempt at distraction, assessing the paintwork as though I'm her apprentice. 'It looks fine to me. But that's not what I meant.'

'I just needed to do something.'

'Of course. And that's great.'

There's a 'but' to follow, yet it remains unspoken, resting silently between us.

'Did we have a session booked in?'

I didn't think she was coming over again until Monday, but it wouldn't be the first time I've confused the date or time of an appointment.

'No. I'm running a lecture on cognitive behavioural therapy this afternoon at UCL.'

'On a Saturday?'

'It's a postgrad course,' she explains. 'Remote learning. They don't have many in-person lectures. I haven't got long, just thought I'd stop by on my way to see how you're doing.'

'I'm not a case study, am I?'

She gives me a wry smile – the kind that says I should know her better than that. 'Is Matt looking forward to tonight?'

'Tonight?'

'The fundraiser this evening. He asked me if I'd like to go with him.'

'Of course. Sorry, he did say.' I'm lying. He didn't mention to me that he'd invited Jess. Or maybe he did, and I just forgot.

'Has he said something to you? About me?'

'We don't talk about you, Suzanna, you know that. The only thing he ever tells me is how much he loves you and wants this to get better.'

This. Like I'm suffering with some kind of ailment. Like bereavement and grief are things that can be smoothed away or manoeuvred past with the right words and sufficient time. Like the guilt can be erased with the right combination of remedies.

'Has he said anything to you about Reka?'

Her brow furrows. 'What about her?'

I glance at the kitchen door, aware that Reka could arrive back at any moment now. 'He's—'

I cut myself short instantly. It feels like a betrayal, to talk to

Jess about Matthew when I have no evidence of any wrong-doing on his part.

'Suzanna... whatever you want to say, you can say to me. Nothing ever goes any further than us, you know that.'

Jess has been my best friend since we met in our first year at the University of Bath. I've always shared everything with her. Most things, at least.

I blurt the truth before I allow myself time to swallow it. 'I think he's attracted to her.'

'To Reka?'

I nod. 'I mean, I wouldn't blame him. I've got nothing to offer him any more. But Noah...'

'Go on.'

'I keep getting this feeling like she's going to try to take Noah away from me.'

Jess sucks in her top lip. 'Has anything happened to make you feel that way?'

You've seen the way she looks at him.

You've seen the way she looks at you.

The gut, Suzanna... don't ignore your gut.

'No.'

Jess exhales as though she's been holding her breath while waiting for my answer. 'This is all normal. I know that doesn't make it any easier for you. But this fear of losing Noah, it's a normal reaction to the loss you've already experienced. Nothing seems secure or stable. The guilt you've spoken about during our sessions... this is your brain's subconscious way of trying to alleviate yourself of its weight for a moment. By transferring the possibility of wrongdoing to someone else, you're lightening the load of your own sense of responsibility. But there are other ways of achieving this... ways you'll come to find easier over time.' She pauses. 'Does this make sense? You can tell me if you think I'm wrong.'

I shake my head. 'No... you're exactly right.'

Her face gives way to her thoughts. She's looking at me, concerned, seeing me in a way that I'm apparently unable to. This is me, not Matthew. This is me, not Reka. I am the problem here.

'Matthew loves you, Suzanna.' Yet the smile she offers me is tight and forced, as though she doesn't truly believe her own words. As though she may need as much convincing as I do.

'Where's Noah?' Jess asks, glancing at her watch.

'Matthew's taken him out.'

I look around at the state of the place, aware of the mess and the chaos. I can offer her a cup of tea, but it'll probably involve milk that's past its use-by date. Reka made a not-so-subtle comment this morning, and when she offered to do the food shop, I didn't have the energy to object. When we hear the front door, both Jess and I assume it's Reka returning from her run. Instead, Matthew and Noah come into the kitchen. Matthew looks surprised when he finds Jess sitting with me at the table.

'Oh, hi. Everything okay?'

'All good. I was just telling Suzanna that I'm giving a lecture at UCL later. I thought I'd pop over to see how you all are before I go. Hi, Noah.'

Noah barely acknowledges her as he goes over to his wooden play kitchen in the corner and retrieves a packet of crayons and some paper from one of its cupboards.

'Soft play?' I mouth, wondering why they're back so soon.

Matthew shakes his head. It was probably too much for Noah on a Saturday. Too many people, and too much noise.

Matthew glances at the clock on the far wall. 'Are you going to have enough time to get ready for this evening?'

'What are you trying to suggest?' Jess says, with mock offence. 'How long do you think I need?' She looks at me. 'Are you sure you don't want to go? It might be a good thing for you to get out for the evening, have a change of scenery.'

She may be right, but the scenery tonight will be exactly the kind I don't need. No doubt there'll be local press there, and I couldn't face being stared at or ignored in equal measure, as though my misery might be caught by anyone unfortunate enough to meet my eye.

'Honestly... not tonight. I'll go somewhere soon, I promise. Small steps, right?'

Jess smiles at Noah as he sits up at the breakfast bar with his colouring things.

'There's no rush,' she says to me. 'But you're sure you don't mind me going instead?'

'Seems a shame to waste a free dinner.'

Jess pushes her chair back. 'I'd better make a move. Am I okay to use your bathroom?'

I nod and she leaves the room, leaving Matthew and me alone. 'She's used to speaking to crowds of students. She'll be so much better at the whole schmoozy networking thing than I am,' he says almost apologetically.

I know he's right. Jess has always had a confidence that's carried her through anything life has put in front of her, and I imagine that tonight, Matthew will rely on her congeniality among strangers to shift the focus from himself.

'You don't have to explain it. It's fine. It'll be nice for you to have the company.'

Better Jess than Reka, which is what he probably would have preferred.

'I didn't know you were planning to decorate,' he says, gesturing to the utility room.

'Neither did I. You don't mind, do you?'

'Of course not. I might go for a run, if that's okay. Wait until I get back and I'll help you with all this.'

He leaves the room to go and get changed into his running gear, but a couple of minutes later I hear his voice on the landing. I leave the kitchen and stand tucked around the corner from the bottom of the stairs, where neither he nor Jess will notice me.

'Her medication,' I hear Jess say. 'There's too much missing.'

'What do you mean?'

'The sleeping pills I prescribed for her... there are too many gone from the box. The same for the Zoloft.'

'You've been snooping around in our things?'

Matthew's voice is blunt, his words clipped.

'Not at all. The bathroom cabinet was open so I went to close it. The boxes are on the shelf.'

Matthew is silent for a moment. I move closer to the bottom of the staircase.

'Has she been doing her own dosage, or have you been giving them to her?'

'What are you suggesting?' Matthew sounds affronted. I've never heard him speak to Jess like this before.

'I just wondered whether she might have got the dosage incorrect somehow. She's been so tired... confused. If she's been accidentally overdosing, that would explain it.'

'It sounded as though you were accusing me of something.'

'Hey,' I say awkwardly as I head upstairs, making no attempt to hide the fact that I've just been listening in on every word. 'I'm sorry,' I say, reaching the landing. 'I didn't mean to be nosy. I just overheard... I...' Matthew's features are taut, his jaw clenched. His eyes fix on me. 'It was me,' I say, looking at Jess. 'I didn't realise. You're right... I've been tired. I must have got mixed up.'

Jess holds my gaze for a moment before looking at Matthew. 'I don't want you to think I was going through your things. But it's important you get the doses right. Maybe you should get one of those days-of-the-week boxes.'

I'm trying not to feel patronised, but it's difficult not to be. Jess looks awkwardly at her watch before saying she'd better be heading off. 'I'll still see you later?' she checks with Matthew, who nods but says nothing.

After she's left, I wait for Matthew to get changed and go out for a run, telling him I'll do some reading with Noah while he's out. But instead of heading back to the kitchen, I go into the bathroom. I click the door shut quietly behind me and go straight for the cabinet above the sink. My boxes of antidepressants and sleeping tablets are on the top shelf, far out of Noah's reach. I take them all out and sit on the edge of the bath as I open each box in turn, counting blister strips and individual pills.

Jess is right: there are too many missing. Far too many.

I know I haven't taken as many as this. I might have made the odd mistake with my dosage here and there, but not to this extent. Jess is right: it would explain how tired and confused I've been. And if I didn't take these pills from their boxes, Matthew must have done it.

FIVE

SATURDAY

His hand is on her arm. It shouldn't matter, this innocent gesture. I suppose it should be a comfort to me that my husband is this kind of person, this type of man: the patient, reassuring kind. He looks good in his suit, ready for the gala that's due to start in a little under two hours. Matthew has always had a way about him that's magnetic to other people, and I knew when I met him that plenty of women found him attractive. I used to dwell sometimes on the thought of how many young, attractive women he must meet at his gyms, but now I fear the threat of temptation lies far closer to home.

I watch them on the driveway from the bedroom window as Reka smiles at him, that wide, natural smile that she gave me the first time she came to our door, not long in the UK from her hometown of Lillafüred in rural northern Hungary. She is pretty when she smiles and she smiles a lot, particularly when Matthew is around. For the first few weeks she was here, I wondered whether she was trying to redress the balance in the house, pushing smiles into corners like pretty ornaments placed on shelves, trying to lift the place from the darkness that hung over us. She knew what she was moving into before she first visited us, and I suppose she had a choice: to counteract our grief with optimism or to get sucked into the shadows, part of the collateral damage of our despair.

His hand is still on her arm. The touch is prolonged now; it means something greater – it has shifted beyond the boundaries of a harmless gesture of solidarity. I watch as he leans into her, his hand moving from her arm to her shoulder. He says something closely, not quite whispered in her ear, but close enough that it suggests a companionship, something secret shared between just the two of them. Yet there's no one around to hear them, anyway. They have no idea I'm here, watching.

She reaches out to him and adjusts his tie. Something is said, and he smiles at her. She laughs.

Reka goes running three times a week: every Tuesday and Thursday evening, and once at the weekend. Her routine remains unbroken; she says the predictability of it is comforting. It gives Matthew and her a common ground that he and I don't have. When we met on a night out nearly seven years ago, we couldn't have been more different in our interests: I liked tea and books and the solitude of libraries, whereas Matthew liked being outdoors regardless of the weather, and he was always socialising, both in and out of work. When he inherited this beautiful house in Kent and the expanse of land that came with it, there'd been the option of selling, but we'd agreed that neither of us wanted to raise our children in London. I'd had a silent concern that the initial sheen of a quieter, rural life would fade in time, and that despite his love of the great outdoors, Matthew would grow to feel isolated. Perhaps that's why he now spends so much time at work. Maybe it's why he now seems so close – too close – to Reka.

She asked me once if I'd ever been a runner, but I haven't been. Not with my legs, at least. I told her I've been running for most of my life: silently, in my head. And never more so than during this past year. She smiled at me, that sad-eyed smile that said she didn't know what to say to that, and I was grateful when she said nothing.

I leave our bedroom and go down the landing and into our son's room. Noah stirs in his bed. It's cold this evening, but despite that, he'll still end up with his spindly limbs shoved above the duvet, arms and legs splayed like a flattened spider. He sweats a lot during the night, something that's only happened over this past year. His dreams are filled with things that frighten him, visions that make him cry out in the darkness, yet he never offers words for what they are, reluctant or unwilling to describe them. My son is a child's drawing of what a boy looks like: a little stick man with a short crop of curly hair, a figure fashioned from pipe cleaners, wiry and flexible. He would curl himself into the tightest of places when we used to play hide and seek. Now, when he hides without wanting to be found, it can take what feels like for ever to find the space into which he has contorted himself.

I should kiss Noah on the head before I leave, whisper a softly spoken night-night into his ear, but I can't. Instead, I pull the curtains closed and leave the room, pulling the door not quite shut so that a shaft of light from the bathroom can fill the crack of space in case Noah should wake up during the night.

Reka is back inside the house. I hear her downstairs, pottering in the kitchen, probably getting herself a glass of water after her run. I stop at the door of Noah's room, rest my fingers on the handle and stay there for a moment, listening for the soft sound of his sleep-filled murmurs. Sometimes it seems that Noah says more during his sleep than he does while awake, his brain betraying his body by letting his secret thoughts escape him.

I am roused from my musings by the sound of shattered glass coming from downstairs. When I go to the kitchen, Reka is on her hands and knees, brushing splintered shards into a dustpan.

'I'm so sorry,' she says. 'I'm so clumsy.'

'It's okay. You're not hurt, are you?'

'No, I'm fine. I'll buy you another glass.'

Her long-sleeved running top has a thin dark line down the back where a perfect trail of perspiration has inched along her spine. The long blonde hair she always wears held back beneath one of her expansive collection of floral headbands is slick with sweat, making it shine beneath the kitchen spotlights.

'You don't need to do that,' I tell her.

She stands and goes to the bin, where she tilts the dustpan and empties the broken glass into the bin bag.

'I was trying to help,' she says, gesturing to the filled sink that is brimming with bubbles and dirty dishes.

'What were you and Matthew talking about?'

She turns sharply, eyeing me with suspicion. She knows now that I was watching them while they spoke outside on the driveway; either that, or she must wonder what else I might be referring to.

'When?'

She has wide eyes, the kind of blue that almost sinks into grey, dark enough to be murky yet not so heavy as to be without that glass-tinged glint that sometimes catches the light when she laughs.

'Outside, just now.'

'Oh.' She smiles. 'He was telling me about tonight. The fundraiser. I don't think he really wanted to go.'

Her accent dances across the words, every sentence lifted at the end as though each statement is a question. Her voice matches her energy and enthusiasm, yet tonight I hear it differently somehow, her intonations seeming to mock me.

'Really? What did he say?'

Reka's mouth curves into a smile, but it doesn't reach her eyes. 'He worries about you.'

I wonder whether this was said just now, or when she called

him yesterday after finding Noah in Annabelle's cot. Perhaps neither is true and the statement is a fabrication, offered to distract me from what's going on right in front of me.

Spoken or not, I feel the words like a sting. I don't want Matthew to worry about me, and if he does, I don't want Reka to be the person to whom he confides about it. He should come to me, yet I know he can't. We can't talk any more, each of us too cautious of the potential violence of own words, both afraid that if we say what we really want to, we will break the other with the truth.

'He doesn't need to.'

I've seen the way he looks at her, and I know he tells her more than he ever says to me. The same probably applies to Noah. I had thought it would help us. I had thought that in our fragile state of brokenness, an unfamiliar and separate presence in our home might somehow help the shape of our fractured family, a kind of human glue that would keep us together when we were most at risk of falling apart. Matthew was insistent that I needed the help. Reka knows little about our lives before she came here; she only knows what she's been told, and we shared our story sparingly, like critics not wanting to offer any spoilers for an audience who had not yet seen the film. We would let her find out for herself. Make her own judgements.

Now, she does judge me. I've seen the looks that are passed my way sometimes. I've heard the barely audible sighs of resignation she has exhaled when she's questioned my behaviour around my son. *My* son. Not hers. Yet I fear she will take him; that she wants my family as her own. Nothing is permanent, not even a life that you brought into being. Life can be snatched from a person while they sleep.

I go to the sink and submerge my hands in the still-warm water.

'Why don't you leave the dishes?' Reka says. 'I'm just going to have a quick shower. I'll do them when I come back downstairs.'

'No,' I say, too quickly. 'It's fine. I'll do them.'

I reach into the suds for a bowl and scrub it more furiously than is needed. I don't want her to think I'm not capable, that I'm losing my grip over the house. I don't want her to think I can't look after my own family.

'Go for your shower.'

Reka opens her mouth to object but changes her mind. I watch her as she leaves, observing the slight curve of her hips and the slenderness of her figure beneath the Lycra running gear she wears. Why wouldn't Matthew want her? Twenty-eight, unruined by pregnancy and childbirth – her youthful optimism still untouched by the cruelty the world has waiting in its shadows.

'Suzanna,' she says, stopping in the kitchen doorway. She looks at me kindly, her face an open page. 'Everything is going to be okay, you know.'

She leaves, not waiting for a response. Her footsteps sound on the stairs, and I wait to hear her bedroom door close before I return my attention to the dishes. I wonder what she makes of us. What she really makes of us. The handsome owner of a successful high-end health and fitness chain. The poor grieving father, saddled with the guilty wife, a negligent mother to their children. He deserves all the accolades and attention he gets. Maybe it's true that he warrants someone more deserving to share his successes alongside him.

I cry out as pain tears through my thumb. When I pull my hand from the sink, the thick washing-up suds are stained pastel pink, a cloud of macabre candy floss. I turn on the tap and run my thumb beneath its flow, yet the blood still pours from the too-deep wound. I put my thumb in my mouth, suckling like a child trying to self-soothe. A metallic tang spreads across my tongue, rusted and bitter. When I put my left hand back into the sink, groping carefully among the plates and cutlery, my fingers meet the offending item. I pull the chopping knife from the water, its blade tipped upwards between the plates.

Reka. She stacked this crockery in the sink. She hid what was in there with a mass of washing-up bubbles; she must have used three times the amount of liquid that was needed. I grab a tea towel from the drawer and wrap it around my thumb before going to the downstairs bathroom cabinet, where the plasters are kept. The wound is deep – it might need gluing – but a couple of plasters will have to do for now.

As I stand in the downstairs bathroom near the bottom of the staircase, I am ripped from my thoughts by the sound of my son's cries. I recognise the agony beyond those wails. I pull the plaster tightly around my thumb as I rush up the stairs and down the landing to Noah's bedroom. The door is open, and a hushed voice drifts from the room.

'Shhhh. Shhhh... everything is okay now.'

In the darkness, Reka is sitting on the edge of Noah's bed. She is still wearing her running clothes, not yet having made it to the shower. My son's head is resting in her lap as her hand strokes his hair, her voice offering the repeated mantra that he is safe now, that everything is going to be okay. In her other hand, she is holding a plastic cup.

'Noah.'

I rush to him, pull him from her grip.

'What are you doing?' I snap accusingly.

'He was crying,' she says defensively. 'He's okay now, aren't you, Noah? It was just a bad dream.'

I pull my son into my body, edging away from Reka. She stands and glances down at the carpet. Guilty.

'What have you given him?' I reach towards her and grab the plastic cup from her hand as its contents slop from its rim on to the train-track rug that lies beside Noah's bed. Soon, he will outgrow the nursery-style décor that we gave his bedroom, his life already so different to the one it was when Matthew and I had stayed up late all those nights with rollers and a pasting table, not wanting to pay someone else to do something we knew we would be proud to have completed ourselves.

'It's just water.'

I don't like the way she is looking at me, as though I've done something wrong by asking her an innocent enough question. If she has nothing to hide, then whatever I ask shouldn't bother her.

Turning my attention to Noah, I adjust the duvet so he's able to move back beneath it. This is a greater length of time than I have held my son in I can't remember how long, and the thought strikes me in the gut like a blade.

'Call me if you need anything,' Reka says, and she leaves us alone. I hum a tune I used to sing when my children were babies, one my mother used to sing to me. Noah is restless for a while, shifting beneath the duvet, too hot despite the cold March evening. I hear the shower running in Reka's en suite bathroom, and a little while later, Noah finally drifts back into sleep.

When I pull the door ajar, Reka is on the landing, about to go downstairs. Her hair is bundled in one of those small towels with a toggle on it, designed specifically to be wrapped around a head. She is wearing a dressing gown and smells of bergamot and lemon; I recognise the scent because I once asked her what perfume she was wearing. She'd told me it was just the body wash she used, and I recall thinking how intoxicating it was.

'Noah's okay now?'

'You won't take him,' I tell her, suddenly. I'm starting not to feel very well; there is sweat running down the back of my neck and my heart is beating too fast, painful in my chest. Perhaps Noah and I have picked up something, although neither of us has really been anywhere. The nursery, I tell myself. They are breeding grounds for viruses.

'No one wants to take your son, Suzanna.'

'I know what you're trying to do. I saw you.'

I think of them together on the drive earlier this evening, smiling as though everything is normal and fine, our lives just like any others. The way she touched him. The way he touched her. I've seen the way Matthew looks at her sometimes, with a longing for something I can no longer offer him. We are too familiar. We have been through too much.

'Suzanna, all I'm trying to do is help you. Matthew was right,' she adds. 'You do need more help.'

A flood of red fills my brain, shooting an angry flare of tinnitus into my ears. He has no right to be talking to her about me.

'Did you do it in our bed?'

Reka's right eyebrow raises in a question mark. 'I'm sorry,' she says, but with the inflection of her accent I can't tell whether it's an apology or an expression of disbelief.

'You and Matthew,' I tell her. 'I know what's going on.'

'Suzanna,' she says, stepping towards me, 'there is nothing going on between Matthew and me.' Her face is flushed – maybe with anger at being accused, perhaps with shame at being caught out.

'Your hair was on his pillow.'

Her face changes. 'And you think that means I slept with him? I made your bed,' she tells me. 'Sometimes, if you're having a bad day, I try to do these things to help you out. Maybe I left the hair there like this.'

Did she make my bed? I've never known her to do this; I've certainly never asked her to.

Sympathy creeps into her features as she watches me question myself. I don't want to see it. I am so sick and tired of people looking at me this way.

'You're lying,' I say quietly, the words barely audible.

'Okay. If that's what you want to believe. You're going to believe what you want anyway.'

I shove past her, bumping into her harder than I'd intended. Reka stumbles back and hits her head on the side of the open bathroom door. She gives a sharp cry of pain and puts a hand to the back of her skull, eyeing me with doubt and disbelief as she nurses her injury. For a moment we stare at each other in shock, neither of us knowing how to act in response. I should speak now, I should say or do something, but I can't. I'd planned to go to my own bedroom, but instead I hurry back to Noah's. I get into bed beside his small, warm body and curl myself around the child I won't let them take from me.

SIX

EARLY HOURS OF SUNDAY MORNING

I stand in the shower with my face tilted to a stream of steaming water. I scrub at my arms with my nails, scouring scratches in my reddened skin, desperate to feel something. To feel anything. I have barely slept. And yet, I must have, because at some point I woke up in my own bed, unable to remember how I got from Noah's room to my own.

I don't know how long I stand in the shower, but when I get out and catch my reflection, my chest is red raw and lined with deep scratches. A few have drawn blood, and yet I don't feel them. I stand with my palms pressed to the sink, forcing myself to look in the mirror. Someone bleary-eyed and burned-out stares back at me. She's a stranger.

Last night's argument with Reka continues to taunt me. The sickness and pain I'd felt in my chest when I'd lain in bed with Noah had subsided after a while, and I realised then that I had taken my fears and frustrations out on her, lashing out for no other reason than that she was available. A hair on a pillow is no proof of anything.

I move away from the mirror quickly, fearful of the woman who continues to stare back. With a towel wrapped around me,

I push open the bathroom window and stand for a moment in the blast of cold air that cools my shower-scorched skin. The window looks out over the wide expanse of garden at the back of the house. There were things I should have finished out there ages ago, before Noah was born. When we first moved here, I was intimidated by the amount of land Matthew had inherited. It was beautiful but too big, and for a while all I foresaw were problems and arguments, financial strains and time constraints.

Over those first few months here, I began to have visions of what it might look like and what it could be. I warmed to the place, starting to believe that this is where we might all grow older – that as a family, we would evolve naturally here, an unexpected forever home. I began to take an interest in gardening, researching the most efficient and easiest ways to establish a garden that would be practical yet in keeping with the rest of the grounds. I vowed to educate myself on the prettiest, hardiest things to grow. There would be a space where I could plant vegetables with the children: they would grow alongside them, an early lesson in patience and persistence and nurture. I'd had time back then to create what I'd imagined, even when I'd believed myself busy. Now, I wonder what I was doing during those days I convinced myself I had no time.

On the mornings when my usual fatigue is replaced by a surge of erratic activity, I've spent the time trying to ready the flower beds for spring. I have sometimes gone out into the garden with a coffee in one hand and a spade in the other and have worked during those still-dark sleepy hours when the rest of the house has yet to rise. When you have a clear enough vision of something, it is easy to work towards it. It's the sketchy, diluted plans that are the trickiest to catch hold of and bring to life.

When I woke this morning, I'd thought for a moment that Noah was in the bed beside me. I put a hand over the curve of his body, turned away from mine, and I pulled myself closer to the warmth of him. But he wasn't there. Matthew's pillow had moved during the night, shifted lengthways like a separate being in the bed. Noah hasn't come into our bed in nearly a year now.

The wound in my hand from the knife in the sink begins to throb, so I go to the cupboard and take out some plasters. I need to get dressed. Before Noah wakes up, I need to speak to Reka. I pushed her. I hurt her. I accused her of something of which I have no proof. And now I have so much making up to do.

I wait until 6.30am to go to her bedroom. The door is partly open, though the curtains are still closed, and it is dark inside the room. I put a hand to the door and stand there for a moment, listening for signs that she's awake. I would usually have heard something from her by this time: movement as she dresses, music playing from her phone, the light tinkle of her laugh as she speaks with a friend or relative from back home. Our altercation last night must have left her exhausted.

'Reka.'

I speak her name quietly as I enter the room. There are clothes strewn over the chair in the corner; mascara tubes and eyeliner pencils scattered across the chest of drawers. A stack of books is piled on the carpet in the corner, and the room smells of wet washing, a used towel presumably left somewhere after her shower last night. Her room is chaotic and messy, in stark contrast with the well-presented, organised persona Reka so expertly exudes. It makes me wonder what else she manages to conceal beneath a façade.

'Reka.'

There is the swell of a body beneath the duvet – the curve of a hip. Her back is turned to me. I wait a moment to see the rise and fall of the duvet as it moves in rhythm with her breathing, still not sure whether she's asleep or just pretending to be so, hopeful that I will leave without her having to speak to me. Either way, I think she can hear me.

'I'm so sorry about last night,' I tell her. 'It was wrong of me.

I hope you can forgive me. I've been under a lot of pressure...
That's no excuse though. I hope you're not hurt. Your head...'

There is the slightest movement in the darkness. She is
listening. She hears my every word. She is punishing me with
silence.

'I'll tell Matthew what happened. What I did. If you want
to leave us, I'll understand, although I obviously hope you
won't. Noah would be devastated.'

The words nearly choke me. Spoken aloud, I realise how
true they are. He is different around Reka, lighter, like a child
should be. Not the world-weary boy he becomes whenever he is
subjected to spending time with me.

'Take the day off,' I tell her. 'Go shopping... go to the cine-
ma... do something nice for yourself. You deserve it.'

She doesn't want to speak to me, and I get it. Perhaps I don't
deserve her forgiveness. Maybe she thinks that this is me, and
what if she's right? This might be who I am now.

'Reka,' I say, in a last attempt to appease her. 'Everything
will be okay, you know.' Her own words offered back to her, as
though they might mean something.

SEVEN

SUNDAY

I can't remember the last time I took Noah to a park. There is one not far from where we live, in the middle of the village close to the local pub, but I don't want to take him there, not wanting to risk bumping into someone we know. Six miles away, in Maidstone, there is a park that backs out on to playing fields. The playground is impressive, recently refurbished with a tall helter-skelter slide, trampolines built into the ground, and a round rope swing large enough to sit six children. It will hopefully be quiet: the weather hasn't been great, and as it's still early there shouldn't be many people there.

I'm taking him to the park. This is progress. Jess says it's a normal reaction, that my inability to dissociate Noah from Annabelle is a natural response that will take time to move away from. She seems confident that it can be done though, and I trust that she is right.

'Would you like to go to the park?' I ask Noah as he chews delicately at the crust of a slice of toast.

I watch my lovely son as he eats, his face pallid, his skin the colour of a scrubbed mushroom.

'Let's try it,' I say, when he offers no response. 'You can let me know if you want to leave.'

I get him dressed, brush his teeth and get him strapped into his car seat. When we get to the park, Noah sits on a bench beside me for a while, eyeballing the playground as though he's carrying out a silent risk assessment.

'Would you like me to push you on the swing?'

Noah turns his head to the row of swings to our right but shakes his head. I wonder what he's thinking. The nursery tells me that he doesn't interact much with the other boys and girls, though they've also made a point of adding that it isn't unusual for children of his age to play by themselves. I think it's more the case that they don't wish to become too embroiled in our issues. They are teachers not psychotherapists; they are no more able to save Noah from the demons that haunt him than I am.

When he finally gets up and heads over to the slide, I am grateful that he has gone. The thought is a selfish one: relief that he is no longer beside me rather than gratitude that he is behaving normally by showing interest in play. Sometimes, just being with him feels overwhelming, a weight of expectation I am not strong enough to bear. My own child. I hear myself, louder than anyone could throw scorn at me for my detachment. I am not fit to be his mother. I am not fit to be anyone's mother. I learned that a year ago.

I watch Noah as he comes down the slide, and I remember how he used to do it, the summer before last when he was still just a toddler. His little voice would give a gleeful 'wheeee', arms raised in the air like someone at the peak of a roller coaster tilted at the cusp of the ride's first drop. Now, his body descends silently and without reaction, his hands at his sides, his mouth fixed firmly in its permanent straight line. I want to wrap him in my arms and hold him until all the hurt is gone, as though by the power of a strong enough, prolonged enough embrace, I might restore him to the child he was before our lives as we'd known them were cut to an end.

Yet I can't even bring myself to be near him. My own son. My firstborn.

Annabelle would have been turning two in early June. She would be twenty-one months old now, on the move and into everything. She would have been able to sit beside Noah in the swings. They would have been able to crawl through the inter-connecting tube tunnels at the far end of the park together, explore the musical pipes at the top of the little climbing frame. She would have followed him like a stray puppy – at times unwanted, at others adored. He would have had a playmate. A best friend for life.

My phone pings in my pocket. I take it out and glance at the screen. There's an email from the head of the company my books are published with. I consider leaving it unread, or waiting to read it later when I'm back home, but curiosity draws me in.

Dear Suzanna,

I hope this email finds you well. Please know, as always, all our thoughts are with you, and I can't reiterate enough that if there's anything you need from us, please reach out and let me know.

Sarah was pleased to receive your email last month, though I don't think she was sent a response to her reply? This is in no way an attempt to hurry you into anything: if you're ready to return to writing, we are of course here to help you, but if not, we will still be here when the timing is appropriate for you. Take all the time you need.

All best wishes,

Lizzy

I'd forgotten all about my email to my editor, Sarah. If she sent me a reply – which she must have done if Lizzy is saying is the case – then I either somehow managed to miss it or I've opened it without reading it. What did I even say to her now? I can't seem to remember.

I search in my sent box for emails to Sarah and find the most recent, sent five weeks ago.

Dear Sarah,

I hope all is well with you. Sorry for not having been in touch for quite some time now. If possible, I'd like to discuss getting back to writing, and to talk over some ideas for the next book. I think it would be a good thing for me to get working again. Could we schedule a meeting when you've got some free time?

Best wishes,

Suzanna

I don't know what I was thinking. I don't have the energy required to write the next in the series. I'm sure that what Lizzy says is entirely true, because surely they would rather wait for me to be in some kind of fit state to produce something worth publishing rather than rush back to work and write a mediocre, half-baked offering. I must have written this email in a fit of pique, longing for an escape from my new normal, desperate for a diversion from the long and silent days that have shaped my life for this past year. But I can't do it. I'm still barely able to think coherently. And at some point, I'm going to have to respond to my editor and admit so.

I look up from my phone and scour the playground for Noah. A flash of a blue coat disappears into one of the tunnels, but when the boy emerges at the end, it isn't my son. I turn my attention to the climbing frame, then the see-saw, then the trampolines. But Noah is nowhere to be seen.

'Noah.'

I get up from the bench and shove my phone back into my pocket. Noah is small; he could be tucked into one of the corners of the boat-shaped climbing frame and from where I've been sitting, I wouldn't be able to see him. When I get to it, I stand on the second rung of the ladder and pull myself up, checking its corners for him. But he's not here.

'Noah!' My voice has raised a pitch, betraying a growing panic. 'Noah!'

The playground has metal fencing running around its perimeter, but the gates are easy enough for even a small child to open. I realise now he could have left while I was looking at that email. There was enough time for him to have done so.

I run to the gate, my heart beginning to thump in my chest. In my head, a silent prayer begins to sound out, desperate and pathetic. *Please don't let anything have happened to my son. I will do anything, just please let him be okay.* This is all my fault. Just like last time, I am to blame. Matthew will never forgive me.

What if someone has taken Noah while my attention was elsewhere? He is the silent child, the boy who doesn't speak; would he even cry out and scream for help if a stranger was to take him by the hand and try to lead him away?

A thought more painful than any other fills my head like a tumour: perhaps he would be grateful to be taken from me. Maybe he would go willingly.

'Noah!'

'Are you okay?'

A young woman holding hands with a toddler in a puddle suit stands at the gate, holding it open for me yet standing in a way that blocks me from being able to pass.

'I can't find my son.'

'Is he wearing a blue coat?' she asks. 'He's just over there, behind the bench.'

I look to where she points and it's now that I see him – or I see his feet, at least, his green trainers with the Velcro straps poking from the end of the bench.

'Thank you,' I say, but I feel her judging me, still watching as I cross the grass to get to Noah. I hear him before I see his face. The sound of his voice nearly stops me in my tracks, though it's not what he's saying that sends a chill to my spine. It's what he is singing.

'La la lu... la la lu.'

He stops when he sees me, the softly sung, barely-there expressions of the lullaby stuttered to a sudden halt.

'Where did you hear that song?' I ask him, my words shaking.

He looks at me with wide eyes. My own son is scared of me.

'You're not in trouble. I just want to know who taught it to you.'

A memory comes back to me, tangible and alive. I am standing in Annabelle's bedroom, nursing my baby with the shock of blue-black hair that every passer-by used to comment on. She is wrapped in one of those little bath towels with a hood, a pair of soft cotton ears flopping either side of her head. She has been fractious for the past four nights, her little cheeks reddened with an assault of first teeth. I hear my voice, low and soothing, the same words that have just now left Noah's lips.

'Where did you hear that song?' I ask him again, but even I can hear how my voice has changed.

I see a lump move in Noah's throat as he swallows. 'Reka.'

The air around us seems to bite at my face. *It's just a coincidence*, I tell myself, *nothing more than a strange coincidence.* Because she could never have heard me sing this song to my daughter. We didn't meet Reka until after Annabelle died.

EIGHT

SUNDAY

When Noah and I get back from the park, Matthew is home. He looks tired. His overnight bag is on the floor in the hallway, next to Reka's running trainers. I ask Noah if he'd like to watch some television while I get him something to eat, and he goes into the living room and settles himself, barely taking up any space on the huge five-seater sofa.

The living room is the first room we completed during the refurbishment of the house. I took such time and effort in choosing the right shade of paint and spent hours scouring the internet for furniture that would be just 'perfect'. I was prepared to spend whatever it took to achieve a dream forever home, yet when I look at it now, I realise how meaningless it all is.

I had never until a year ago realised how little money meant. Over the course of my adult life, my income had been a series of things: a goal that was set and worked towards, an inconvenience that withheld from me the life I'd wanted, a wily, changeable thing that I grasped at like a fisherman trying to snare a slippery catch. And then it became what I'd assumed was the winning ticket: financial security, the means by which everything else would magically fall into place.

I had written two books while still in my twenties: a double attempt at the kind of domestic dramas I loved to read in my spare time. Somehow, I'd managed to find myself an agent. The books were signed by a publisher, but neither of them sold well. I was dropped by the publisher, parted ways with the agent. I'd always been aware that writing as a career was a risky and unstable ambition. For a time, I stopped writing altogether. And then I watched a documentary about a detective who'd worked on a case involving a mysterious call from a wife to her husband, during which he had listened to her abduction taking place. That night, I couldn't stop thinking about the possibilities of what might have happened to her, an entirely different outcome with a succession of twists playing out in my head like a full-length feature film. I'd got up from bed in the early hours to write everything down, not trusting my brain to recall the details by the time morning arrived. From there, the first in my series of police procedural novels was born. I was offered two contracts on the same day, signed with a new publisher, and the book hit number one in the UK Kindle charts, sitting there for over three weeks. The first in the series went on to sell over a million copies, and it changed my life overnight.

Looking back now, I realise there was an arrogance to my assumption that financial security would cement my life with the kind of happiness that had always felt elusive to me. Suddenly I had everything I'd ever wanted: a career that allowed me to live immersed in my creativity, a successful husband who supported my dreams and shared my values, a perfect son who had made us a family. And then, not too long later, a beautiful daughter who had made our family complete. For nine months, the four of us lived in what to anyone else may have appeared an idyllic, exhausted, familial bliss, and I'd naïvely believed that this was it: the start of forever. But it was only the beginning of the end.

I stand in the living room doorway and look at Noah, curled into a foetal position at the end of the sofa. He looks like he did yesterday, when Reka and I found him in Annabelle's cot, and I try to shake the image from my mind as I look at him. His eyes are heavy, and his face always pales when he's tired. I get a blanket from the ottoman and place it over him, and he barely stirs in response.

'I'll just be in the kitchen if you need me.'

When I get there, Matthew is sitting at the breakfast bar drinking a coffee. He looks tired. 'Hey,' he says as I enter the room. 'I wondered where you were.'

'I took Noah to the park.'

'Is he okay? Where is he?'

'Needs a nap. He's on the sofa.'

'Would you like one?' he offers, and for a moment I think he's referring to a nap. *There is nothing I'd like more*, I think. I can't remember the last time I slept for longer than a couple of hours at a time, not woken by vivid dreams or sounds that seemed to grow from beneath the nightmare.

He gestures to the mug in front of him. 'Suzanna? Coffee?'

I nod and go to sit next to him.

'How did last night go?' I ask him, because this is what we're supposed to do – move through the motions of everyday normalness until something shifts and settles.

'Fine,' he says, going to the coffee machine.

'That's it? Just fine?'

'Not much more to say about it,' he says, keeping his head turned from me. 'I got through it.'

He finishes making coffee and brings a cup over to me, placing it on the table. When he sits in the chair next to me, he reaches out and puts his arms around me in a way he's not done in a long time, pulling me closer.

'I'm glad you went,' I tell him. 'You needed it. It was the right thing to do, for them and for you.'

A waft of perfume catches in the back of my throat. I don't recognise its scent; it doesn't belong to me.

'I wish you'd come with me.'

He holds me too tight, until it feels claustrophobic. I pull away from him and get up to go to the fridge, taking out butter and ham and tomatoes, trying to distract myself from the scent that still lingers in my nose. By the time I've made Noah a sandwich, he will have gone to sleep, but I need to busy myself with the task to distract myself from Matthew.

'Did Jess enjoy it?'

'What?'

'The gala. Did she have a good night?'

Matthew doesn't answer. When I look at him, he's looking down at his phone. I'm not sure he's even heard my question.

'Matt.'

'Sorry... what?'

'Did Jess have a good night?'

'As far as I know. We didn't see much of each other... you know what these things are like.'

I don't, but I let the comment slide. For whatever reason, Matthew doesn't seem to want to share the details of last night. Perhaps he's just relieved it's over. Attention wasn't what he'd been looking for when he'd started working on the fundraising project. In a situation where he'd lost all control and had no power to reverse our new reality, I think he craved a feeling that he was doing something helpful for someone. Anyone.

My mind drifts back to Noah and the song I heard him singing at the park. I consider telling Matthew about it, but he will only think me paranoid for even contemplating it as anything more than a coincidence. I know it means nothing, yet it was somehow haunting, those words sung so deliberately by my son who barely says a word from one day to the next. It was like hearing the lullaby from within a dream, or perhaps some kind of nightmare.

I cut the sandwich into four and put two pieces on one of Noah's plastic plates, one with a circle of tiny trains and tractors. I slice some apples and cheese and put them alongside it, but when I take it to the living room, Noah is asleep, his chest rising and falling gently. I hope he doesn't dream. I hope for his sake that his sleep spares him from the kind of images that wake me in the small hours during which everything appears at its most horrifying.

When I take his lunch back to the kitchen to cover it with cling film for later, Matthew is in the utility room unloading the washing machine. He has one of Reka's running tops in his hands. 'This has just been left here,' he says. 'Has she gone out?'

'I'm not sure.'

Matthew throws the top back into the machine and sighs. It occurs to me that perhaps Reka has started wearing perfume. Maybe it transferred from something belonging to her when Matthew moved it out of his way. As innocent as a hair left on a pillow after changing bed linen.

'She needs to clear up after herself. This stuff's starting to smell.'

'It's not a problem,' I tell him, reaching to the top shelf for the box of washing powder. 'I'll just run it through again.'

'You shouldn't be doing her washing for her, Suzanna. She's supposed to be here to help you, not the other way around.'

'She's not a cleaner.'

'It's her own stuff. She needs to deal with her own stuff.'

I tip some washing powder into the machine's tray, turn the dial to thirty degrees and press the start button. I know Matthew is right, but I'm grateful that Reka isn't here this afternoon. Noah and I needed the time alone together, just the two of us, and had Reka been here when Matthew had got home, she'd likely have told him about our argument last night. After seeing them together on the driveway yesterday evening, I'm still not sure whether I can trust her, despite what she said last night. I'm not sure I can trust anyone any more.

'You've got your appointment with Jess tomorrow,' he says, and I can't make out whether it's said as a statement or a question.

'In the morning, while Noah's at nursery.'

Matthew says nothing. The building whirr of the washing machine breaks the silence between us. Sometimes, during these quiet moments, I wonder at the extent to which Matthew must try to decode me. More recently, it seems that at some point he will start to give up on his attempts to work out what's going on inside my head.

'You still think it's the right thing for you... speaking to Jess?'

'Why wouldn't it be?'

'No reason. I'm just checking.'

'Do you think it's time to talk to her together?' I ask him. I'd mentioned joint sessions when the subject of therapy first arose, but Matthew dismissed it, for that time, at least. Everything he said in objection to the idea made sense, and I knew he was right when he'd said that I would never be able to properly open up about the things I was feeling while he was sitting in the room beside me. There have been things I've said to Jess that I would never have been able to give voice to had Matthew been there. My admissions would have led to anger and resentment, and so now we must continue to play out the respective roles we each have in this marriage, acting our parts until one of us slips up and forgets our lines.

'Perhaps. But not with Jess.'

After reading various articles online, I realised that having Jess as my therapist was going against one of the basic rules of counselling, which is not to be led by anyone known to the family. But Jess is my oldest and closest friend. That's what makes it work. I could never have confided in a stranger about the thoughts and nightmares that have plagued me over this past year in the way that I have with Jess.

'It's been a year,' I needlessly remind him. If Matthew doesn't talk about our daughter soon, I'm starting to wonder whether he'll ever be able to.

'Exactly. A year. It's no time at all. Grief doesn't have a timeframe.'

His eyes are pale and watery. He looks away, his teeth clamping down on his bottom lip. He won't allow himself to cry, not when he knows my own tears are always bound to follow. I'm never sure if it's for my sake or for his.

'Matthew.'

'It's okay,' he says, raising a hand. 'I'm okay. I'm sorry.'

'You don't have to be sorry. I just wish we could talk about her.'

Matthew shakes his head, trying to silence me. I can't remember the last time he spoke Annabelle's name. We don't share anecdotes about the funny gurgling noises she used to make with her dummy at night or talk about the heart-shaped birthmark on her left thigh. We don't laugh about the way she used to try to feed herself with her spoon turned upside down. We don't reminisce about the sleepless nights that at the time felt like a relentless test of endurance but have since become the halcyon days we took so carelessly for granted. We never sit and smile at details of the day of her birth or lie together and cry about those from the day she was buried, her tiny wooden coffin lowered into the same plot shared by my parents.

I am standing here silently pleading with him to talk to me about her, but he still can't bring himself to do it.

When he moves towards me, I think for a moment that he might pull me into him as he did just earlier in the kitchen. I picture us clinging to one another, our bodies slumping to the floor as we allow ourselves to be gripped by our mutual grief, the weight and intensity of it dragging us to the cold tiles and keeping us there until we are drained of the things we have kept caged inside us. Instead, he reaches behind me to the top of the washing machine and picks up the bottle of fabric conditioner, returning it to the high shelf, out of Noah's reach. The good parent. The practical, safe one.

'Would you like me to speak to Reka?' he asks.

'About what?'

'Her things. The fact she needs to pull her weight a bit more. I don't mind doing it, but one of us has got to.'

'No,' I say, a little too quickly. 'It's fine. I'll do it.'

Matthew doesn't need more reason to spend time in Reka's company. I suspect he is already around her more than I realise, her unspoiled psyche a tonic to neutralise the despair his wife brings.

I watch him as he stares at her pile of washing, his gaze remaining on her things a little longer than it should.

'Let's have dinner together tonight just the three of us,' he suggests, snapping his focus from Reka's clothing as he realises that I've noticed it. 'What do you reckon?'

Since Reka arrived in our lives, we have always included her in the routine aspects of our day, and she has been welcomed at every mealtime. We'd agreed that while she lived in our home, she should be treated like a member of the family. Although grateful for our offers, Reka has mostly kept herself separate. I'd thought that perhaps she finds it more professional to maintain a distance, respectful of the time alone we have as a family, although seeing her with Matthew as I did on the driveway yesterday, I'm no longer convinced this is the reason.

'I'll text Reka and let her know,' I say.

Guilt, the voice in my head tells me. He has suggested tonight out of guilt.

He leans in and kisses me gently on the forehead before leaving me alone in the utility room, the rumble of the washing machine a soundtrack to the film that plays out in my head.

There's a hotel room, an opened wine bottle on a bedside table; two glasses stand beside it, both nearly empty. There are crisp white sheets and muted lighting: Matthew in the suit he wore to the event last night; Reka, naked on the bed. The scene plays out in high definition, every inch of skin and murmur of pleasure as real as though they are in front of me. I close my eyes, put my hands over my ears.

Don't stop, I hear her tell him, her voice as clear as though she were standing behind me.

But I know this didn't happen. She was here, with me and Noah.

Yet in the reel my mind continues to play out, he follows her instruction and doesn't stop. And despite my every effort, I can't make the images or the sounds stop either.

NINE

MONDAY

For the past six months I have met with Jess for a therapy session once a week. I went over to her house for our very first session, and I sat in the back room she uses for meeting with clients. For the entire hour, I froze. I'd known this woman for years – she'd been in my life for longer than anyone else – yet I couldn't bring myself to even open my mouth. There were a million words soaked into my tongue, but they had become so absorbed there that I didn't know how to release them into the air. But as Jess later told me, it was her job to find a way to do that.

I'd feared that having her try to pick apart the intricacies of my brain might alter our friendship. I didn't want to come to resent her or to feel shame whenever we were in the same room, yet all these concerns were allayed when she suggested that she see me at home rather than making me travel to her. The effort of simply readying myself to leave the house was such that by the time I got to her place, I already felt that half my reserves had been depleted. But with Reka absent this morning, I'd needed to make myself presentable enough to take Noah to nursery. Now, Jess and I sit in the smaller of my home's two reception rooms, me on the sofa, Jess in the wide armchair by the front window.

She has the kind of voice that could lull you into a deep and dreamless sleep, and when she looks at me, she does so with the face of someone listening because she wants to and not purely because she's paid to put up with the emotional outpourings of the people who settle themselves opposite her and allow their grief to spill forth like tea shared between friends. I know her well enough to know that this is how she is with all her clients. For Jess, her career is her life's calling, not just the means by which she pays her bills and mortgage.

'Would you like a drink before we start?' she asks me, in the same way she begins every session. She knows the house well enough to know where everything is. On my worst, weakest days, I have allowed her to carry on in the kitchen, grateful to her for taking over and leading where I can't. Sometimes pride forces me to play host, embarrassed at the thought that I can barely function enough to produce a cup of tea and a plate of biscuits. But today, I have insufficient energy for pride.

'I should have got it ready before you arrived.'

She waves a hand to dismiss my apology, and she goes to the kitchen, returning minutes later with a pot of tea and two mugs.

'How has your week been?' she asks as she settles into the chair.

'I spent some time with Noah yesterday, just the two of us.' I omit the detail of having momentarily feared I'd lost him in the park while distracted by my phone. She presumably already thinks me a terrible mother, regardless of her loyalties to me.

'Did he speak to you?'

'No. He was singing though.'

'Okay. This sounds like progress. What was he singing?'

I hear his voice in my head, quiet and haunting, barely muttering those seemingly innocent lyrics. 'It was a lullaby.'

'One you used to sing to him?'

I shake my head. 'My mother used to sing it to me when I was little. My grandmother had sung it to her. It's that one from *Lady and the Tramp*... the Peggy Lee song. I could never bring myself to sing it to Noah... it was too emotional. But somehow, I was able to sing it to Annabelle.'

Jess is quiet for a moment. She sits with one leg over the other, her hands clasped together on her knee. She's the same age as I am – thirty-eight – but she's always looked younger than her years. Her style is youthful, her make-up minimal but applied with an assuredness. For as long as we've known each other, I've never seen her in clothing that is anything but block colours: today, a khaki button-down dress and a pair of flat-heeled ankle boots.

'Noah's obviously a bright child, to recall that lullaby having been so young himself.'

I smile as though in gratitude for her compliment to my son, when really, I'm holding back the reaction my body longs to set free. Noah doesn't remember that song: it is impossible. That tune was for Annabelle's ears only, a song my mother had sung to me, its lyrics therefore cemented in my mind as ones intended for a daughter from her mother. I sang other songs to Noah, songs that meant as much, but that one alone was for Annabelle and me.

I reach for my mug, and it shakes in my hands.

'How did you feel?' Jess asks, shifting in her chair. 'When you heard that lullaby?'

'I was shocked,' I admit. 'I hadn't realised Noah knew it.' I don't want to tell her about Reka; I've already said too much where she's concerned. She must already think me paranoid after my comment about Reka and Matthew, and paranoia arouses suspicion. Grief is forgivable. It can be understood and empathised with. A person's grief can be moulded to fit into different-sized boxes; in the right hands, it is malleable and can be contained under some element of control. Paranoia is different. It is a slippery, malignant thing – feared by those who know of its presence, an invisible threat to those who don't.

'Did you feel any different towards Noah, after spending time together yesterday?'

'Guilty,' I tell her, the word slipping easily from my tongue. 'He's just a child. I want him to be happy. He deserves to be happy.'

'And you? Do you think you deserve to be happy?'

I chew the inside of my bottom lip. Jess's focus upon me feels intense as she waits for an answer that I'm unable to give her.

'Do you think that being happy would be a form of betrayal?'

'I suppose so,' I admit. 'In a sense.'

'Tell me about the last time you were happy. Do you remember it?'

I can't. I don't remember what happiness sounds or tastes like, or how it feels between my fingers. There is a moment each morning when for the slightest fraction of a second, I wake and feel nothing. There is a split second before reality presses its weight down upon me, and in that briefest slice of time, that moment of oblivion, I suppose this is the closest thing to how happiness might feel.

'I don't know,' I tell her absently, my head beginning to hurt.

'Was it before or after Annabelle was born?'

She looks at me apologetically, sorry for having to ask the question. When she'd mentioned postnatal depression to me in those first weeks following Annabelle's birth, I'd already known there was something wrong. I hadn't felt myself, but it was so much more powerful than that. I wasn't sure I even remembered what it felt like to be me. Now, I understand the implication of her question. It saddens me to think that, maybe, Annabelle's short nine months of life were shaped by a sadness

into which she'd been born, and that I was unwittingly responsible for that.

'I'm not sure,' I admit.

'When you think of her, what do you think of?'

Jess meets my eye. She gives me a silent look of encourage-
ment, and I feel tears pinch, threatening to escape me. I think
she already knows the answer. We've touched upon it so many
times, though I've never been able to speak the full truth aloud.
I've never been able to admit to her – I've never really been able
to admit to myself – that when I think of Annabelle, all I'm able
to see is the way she was that afternoon, on the day she left our
lives.

'I worry I'll forget her,' I say, avoiding an entirely honest
answer to the question. 'The smell of her skin, the sound of her
cries... What if one day I can't recall these things, or I remember
them differently to how they really were?'

'Does that happen to you? Do you often remember things
differently to how they really were?'

'I don't know. I suppose I wouldn't though, would I? Otherwise, I'd be remembering them correctly, if that makes sense.'

Jess twists the ring that sits on the third finger of her right
hand. She is unmarried; she's had a few casual boyfriends over
the years, and one more serious relationship that ended eigh-
teen months ago. Matthew and I met him on a few occasions,
but things didn't work out between them, and Jess didn't seem
too disappointed when they decided to separate. Jess has always
been so devoted to her job and driven by a desire to help others
that she's never really seemed to have the time for a committed
relationship.

'Is her bedroom still the same?' she asks me.

I nod. No one else goes in there, though I know Matthew
doesn't believe it healthy to keep our daughter's things as they
were when she was still alive. Maybe he's right. Yet I can't bring
myself to change anything. The crocheted blanket one of my

cousins made for her and sent in the post from Italy still hangs over the end of the cot, left there after Annabelle's last nap. The baby record player with the gramophone speaker that plays tiny plastic records is still set up on the dressing table, the last set of songs we listened to together still resting on the turntable. The last Babygro she wore to bed is folded on the mattress.

'Does being in the room with all her things as they were help you to remember?' Jess asks.

'Sometimes. Other times, it almost seems to have the opposite effect. It's like my brain shuts down and it won't allow me to see or hear her.'

'Self-preservation. Your brain's way of protecting you from further trauma.'

As she's done on other occasions, Jess reaches into her bag and pulls out a box of tissues. She places them on the wooden coffee table between us. As is mostly the case, they will remain untouched. The tears Jess expects to be shed in this room during our sessions are continually absent. I try to think of the last time I cried, but I can't recall it. Crying requires an energy of which I no longer seem to be in possession.

'The guilt,' I say. 'The guilt is never going to go away.'

I wait for Jess to say something, but she doesn't. I know that therapists aren't meant to pass opinion, that they listen and guide, trying to help you find your own solution to a problem. But for this, there is none. And perhaps there's a part of me that wouldn't yet be ready to hear it.

The silence seems loud, a ringing in my ears flaring like a klaxon and then not letting up. I feel my jaw tense as I try to push away the din, but it simply evolves, escalating to a painful crescendo. To break it, I speak, desperate for the noise to stop. I say something I've never been able to admit aloud before.

'It was my fault. I killed her.'

TEN

MONDAY

By the time Jess leaves the house, I am physically and emotionally exhausted. Our sessions seem to have this effect; after them, I feel as though I've completed an assault course during which my body has been pelted with rocks. I go to collect Noah from nursery, barely registering the teacher's words when she tells me something about how things have been this morning. We drive home in our usual silence, and when I let us into the house, I tell him to go to his room and choose some books to take to Reka.

I go into the back garden, to the summer house that Matthew had converted to a writing room for me six months before I found out I was expecting Noah. It is fully equipped with heating and broadband; I could move into the place if necessary, and on the long nights in the build-up to a deadline, I was known to fall asleep in my chair, awoken by Matthew's hands on my shoulders rousing me from dreams.

I turn on my laptop and go to my emails, reading over those sent by Lizzy and Sarah at the publishing house. A sickness churns in my gut, and my temples are pulsing with the threat of a migraine. I should have made myself something to eat before I came out to the garden. Did I have anything at breakfast? I can't seem to remember.

Dear Lizzy, I start to type. *Thank you for your email.*

I sit back and stare at the screen as the words blur in front of my eyes. I know that something should follow, some kind of response to what has already been said, but for whatever reason, I can't push the words from my head to my hands. My fingers linger over the keys, waiting for me to prompt them into action. Together, we sit here inert and wordless.

It is warm in the summer house, the early spring sun flooding through the windows and illuminating the dust particles that float like fairies around me. I will need to spring clean. Declutter. Try to lighten my mental load, as though a mind can be cleared as easily as everyday excess.

When I open the door, a welcome breeze fills the space. I hear Noah's laugh instantly, as though it has been waiting at the door to be allowed in. It skirts along the blinds and lifts the papers on my desk, curling them at the corners like smiles. The sound sits in my gut, settling there like a stone dropped into murky pond water, its ripples still visible on the surface. It should make me happy. But I don't know how to be happy any more.

I return to my desk, switching my focus back to the single line of text I have managed to produce. I delete it and start again, as though a second attempt at an introductory phrase will manage to spur into life a full paragraph, something worthy of clicking the send button. It doesn't.

There is another burst of laughter. I see a flash of red sweater as Noah races towards the climbing frame at the far side of the garden. It's been so long since I saw him run anywhere; so long, in fact, that I'm sure he hasn't in nearly a year. For a while, time stopped. Noah stopped with it. Since then, he has moved through life as though wading through mud, his little feet suckered to the ground. Nothing piques his interest any more. There is no longer anything that can excite him.

He will spend hours on the swing that hangs from the climbing frame, though. Often, if he disappears from the house, this is where we'll find him, his hands gripping the thick rope tightly, his little knuckles white with the determination of not falling. Everything he does now is deliberate: each step taken like an elderly man unsteady on his feet, each mouthful of food paused at his lips before it is tasted. In every action there is a result or a consequence, and Noah now exists at four years old acutely aware of each and every one, realising already that danger surrounds him.

When I pull my thoughts from Noah and return them to the screen, I am further away from being able to write a response to my publisher. I go back to my sent box and search for the email I sent to Sarah, the one in which I stated a readiness to return to writing. My own words mock me from the screen. They are asking me whether I'm ready to start writing another book; by all accounts, I've volunteered myself available to the idea. Yet I can't even construct an email.

Reka's voice rises in a crescendo from the garden. I've heard them play this game before. There's a series of hand claps and then a pause. Reka calls him once, twice, three times. The inflection of her accent raises his name in the middle, the vowels lifted as though in song.

'Noah. Noah. Nooooo-aaaaah.'

Stop it, I think. *Stop calling his name.*

The two of them shriek as she chases him in the garden, and I should be happy, I know I should – this is how his life should be, unburdened by the weight of a trauma his little life could never have been prepared for. I could go outside and join them, but I know the laughter and the fun would stop, struck dead as though killed by a blade with my presence. I don't want to be guilty of killing their enjoyment, not when I am already so responsible for the death of so much.

'Nooooo-aaaaaah.'

Her voice fills my ears and floods my brain. I stare at the screen, at the email I sent to Sarah, the words alien to me. Reka's voice sounds again, and I clamp my hands over my ears, unable to drown her out.

Please, I think. *Shut up, shut up, shut up.*

And then, amid Reka's calls and Noah's laughter, managing to push through the palms that cover my ears, there comes another sound. A baby crying.

I know it is her because her sound is distinct – to me, at least. Put a mother in a room full of wailing infants and she will be able to identify her child from among them; that persistent, shrill pitch is nature's alarm, a siren that cannot be left ignored, each cry with its own unique timbre and rhythm. I hear her, but I cannot reach her. I am unable to see her, to picture her in my mind's eye as though she were here.

As the sounds from the garden grow louder, so do Annabelle's cries. Reka's voice rises... Noah's laughter grows piercing... The cries come quicker and more closely together, barely a break between them.

Please, I think. *I'm sorry, I'm sorry, I'm sorry.*

I shove my chair back and get up to slam the door of the summer house, the pane of glass trembling as the door clicks shut. There is a pounding in my head, the rush of a river, and my heart is stuttering in my chest, desperate to settle. I press my forehead to the door's glass and close my eyes, using one of the breathing techniques Jess has taught me to try to help deal with the onslaught of a panic attack.

One, I count in my head. *Two, three, four...*

The sound of the crying subsides. It fades into the echo of a murmur, and then it is gone. There is silence. I exhale slowly and heavily, my shoulders sagging with the effort. When I open my eyes, the sky has darkened. A gathering of grey clouds threaten rain.

Noah's red sweater is on the ground at the bottom of the climbing frame. *He'll be cold*, I think, but then I realise he's still wearing it.

I yank the door open and run to Noah, who is splayed in a heap on the grass. His right leg is at an awkward angle, and his left hand is holding the side of his head. At first, I think he's unconscious, but then I hear a soft whimpering sound.

'Noah.'

I scoop him up in my arms, my weightless slip of a child, and when I put my hand over his, I pull it away to find my fingers smeared with warm blood.

'Noah,' I say, trying to keep the panic from my voice, 'I need you to let me see.'

He moves his hand away, his arm dropping limply at his side as he turns his face towards my chest. There is a wound at the side of his head, an inch wide and spilling crimson.

Oh God, there is so much blood.

'Where is Reka?'

But it is pointless asking him, and it doesn't matter. She isn't here. She has fled from us, and I wonder whether I'm to blame for it. Perhaps she fears me as much as my son seems to.

I carry him to the house and go into the kitchen, grabbing a clean tea towel from the drawer. I hold it to his head, covering the injury, then in the hallway I find our coats and shoes, still carrying Noah slumped like a sack on my shoulder.

'Come on, let's get you into the car.'

Noah cries as I clip him into his car seat and instruct him on how to hold the tea towel over the wound. My hands are shaking as I start the car and leave the driveway. I glance at my son in his car seat, his crimson blood spattered on his pillar-box sweater. Social services will come here; if not tomorrow, then the next day. They will ask questions I don't have answers for. They will think me unfit all over again.

ELEVEN

MONDAY

I call Matthew on the way to the hospital, but he doesn't answer. I thought he might have finished work by now, but perhaps he's been held up. He always tends to be busier in the mornings than in the afternoons, and though each of his gyms has its own manager and team of staff, Matthew likes to be seen as a regular presence.

'Matt,' I say when the answerphone kicks in, 'there's been an accident. Noah's had a fall. I'm taking him to A&E.'

In the back, Noah has fallen asleep in his car seat. I call his name to try to rouse him, unable to remember whether you're supposed to let a child fall asleep after a head injury or whether the guidance on that has changed. There are so many things to be aware of where children are concerned: rashes and temperatures, tummy aches and allergies. Parenting requires an encyclopaedic knowledge of symptoms and remedies beyond the capabilities of most average people.

Average. We are certainly not that. Another ambition achieved, it would seem, because what person ever sets out with an aim for normality? I wanted better than average, in every aspect: my career, my home, my family. Now, normal is everything I would kill for.

When I reach the hospital, I remember how difficult it is to park here, and after looping floors and floors of a dingy multistorey, I abandon the car on double yellow lines just opposite the entrance of the A&E department. Noah wakes when I unclip him and pull him from his car seat, and he starts to cry – tiny, plaintive whimpers that turn heads as I carry him into the building and to the front desk.

'My son's had a fall,' I tell the woman sitting behind the glass, and she proceeds to take his name and date of birth before asking me for details of what happened.

I become acutely aware of the people sitting just behind us, so close that they're unable to do anything but listen to my description of events. The woman at the front desk remains impassive, her features barely moving while she looks at me. Noah's crying escalates, turning from whimpers to full blown howls. I hear someone behind us curse under his breath when Noah and I are shown to a side room by a male nurse.

'Let's take a look at you, little man,' he says kindly as he pushes Noah's curls aside to assess the injury beneath. He asks me to go through what happened again, and so I do. I mention Reka, of how she was meant to be looking after him. Noah is still crying. It occurs to me that I should in some way be grateful for the sound, with it so rare that he makes any. But this is not how I want to hear him. Not in pain and suffering like this.

'Quite a nasty fall you've had there,' the nurse says, giving Noah a smile. 'Nothing a bit of glue won't sort out.'

Relief swells in my chest. The injury had looked so serious when I'd first lifted Noah from the ground and then touched his head to find his blood on my fingers. My head had been filled with visions of surgeons and recovery, my son scarred for life or left with a permanent injury.

'There was so much blood,' I say to no one in particular.

'Head injuries do a good job at scaring us,' the nurse says, getting up from his seat. 'It's not a bad one though. I've seen a lot worse.'

He disappears out into the corridor, and I take my phone from my pocket to check whether Matthew has yet been in touch. No missed calls. No messages. Resentment curls in my chest at the thought of what he might be doing that could be more important than this, than us, than his family.

The thought that he might be somewhere with Reka stabs me in the gut. What if he already knows what happened, if she went straight to him and let him know her version of events, not allowing me a chance to get the truth in first? I see her crying to him, apologising... his hands on her shoulders as he tells her it was only an accident.

The nurse returns and shows us to another room. Thankfully, Noah's cries have subsided, and he is silent now, his head lolled on my shoulder as I carry him along the corridor. There is blood on my sweater that must have got there earlier; it has dried in a hard scab that has crinkled the fabric. The staff are pleasant and helpful, tending to Noah with patience and kindness, but I barely register what is being said and done around us. The last time I was in a hospital, I was leaving Annabelle behind. Now, just the smell of the place takes me back to that day.

Once the wound has been glued and I've been handed some paperwork about aftercare, Noah and I head back to the car. He's still exhausted, so I carry him from the hospital. As we leave the main entrance, I hear Matthew calling my name.

'Is he okay?' he says breathlessly, running towards us. He takes Noah from me as soon as he reaches us, and I hate myself for not resisting. Why have I allowed my child to be pulled from my arms like that?

'Hey, mate.' Matthew ruffles Noah's hair gently, searching for the injury. 'What happened?'

'He fell,' I tell him when Noah says nothing.

'Where the hell was Reka?' Matthew asks, turning his question away from Noah's ears. 'Why wasn't she with him?'

He might be naming Reka, but I know I'm the one he's blaming, and he's right to hold me responsible. Noah may have been in her care at the time, but I was still there. I should have been present.

'She was,' I say, not intending to sound so defensive. 'But... I don't know... She must have run off when he fell.'

'Run off?' Matthew's face is flushed with anger. I've rarely seen him like this. 'She's supposed to look after him – that's the whole point in her being there!' He adjusts Noah on his shoulder and gets his phone from his pocket with his free hand. 'She can pack her stuff tonight,' he says.

'Matt—'

'It's not up for discussion. I can't believe you'd even consider keeping her with us after this. I wouldn't have blamed her for the accident – kids have falls all the time – but to just go and leave him when he was hurt? It's unforgivable.'

I see her name on his screen before he tries to call her. His reaction to her absence seems extreme, his protest against her overly forceful. Is this a convincing act, performed to distract me from the idea of them having been together? Have they argued, and this now gives him an opportunity to get her gone from our home?

'Straight to answerphone,' he says, lowering the phone from his face. 'How convenient.'

He shoves his phone in his pocket. 'Where are you parked?'

I gesture to the A&E department. 'Just over there.'

'He can come with me,' Matthew says, even though my car is closer.

I open my mouth to object, but Matthew cuts me short.

'Tell her she needs to pack her things. You do it, or I will.'

TWELVE
LATE MONDAY NIGHT

The baby is crying again. She is always crying. Her desperate wails, a most pitiful sound, crash along the landing from the nursery and burst into the room in fits of noise that are echoed on the monitor on my bedside table. I get out of bed bleary-eyed and sleep-worn, and I go down to her room to settle her. When I get there, the night light on her chest of drawers is on, casting a pale orange glow across the end of the cot. The sound grows louder, shrill and insistent. Yet when I lean into the cot to lift her from the mattress, her mouth is shut. With her perfect little rosebud lips clamped together, she looks as though she is deep in sleep. Yet the sound of her cries still rings in my ears. And she isn't sleeping. She is dead to the world.

The sheet beneath her head is stained bright red, a macabre flower that spreads from her skull. My hands reach for the sides of her head, lifting her gently as the noise that cocoons us rises to a screaming peak. There is blood on my fingers, smeared across my wedding ring and splashed over my knuckles. There is a gaping wound at the back of her skull, spilling red.

I let her go. I stand over my beautiful, bloodstained baby and I listen to her screams until I realise no sound comes from her and the noise is mine alone, dragging me from this nightmare.

A hand pushes pressure on my shoulder, shaking me awake. 'Suzanna. It's okay.'

Our bedroom is a square of shapes in the darkness as my eyes adjust to the familiarity of the furniture. It was a nightmare. Just a nightmare. One that doesn't end when I'm switched into wakefulness.

Matthew's hand rests on my shoulder, the cold pad of his thumb gently moving back and forth across my bare skin. I feel the chill of his wedding band. 'It's okay,' he says again, but it is not okay. Nothing will ever be okay again.

'Do you want to talk about it?' he offers, already knowing the answer. I never want to share the details of what happens in my nightmares.

'No. I'm fine.'

He moves closer behind me and slips his arm around my waist. I feel myself flinch involuntarily, unused to him so close to me, the heat of his bare chest pressed against my back. I can't remember the last time we were this close. His stubble scratches the back of my neck as his lips find my skin. I lie still, not knowing how to respond. His touch feels familiar yet alien, comforting yet somehow invasive.

The arm around my waist moves, and his fingers push beneath my T-shirt, finding my stomach. They trace up to my breasts, passing across my skin so lightly they barely touch me. His other arm pushes beneath me. The fingertips of his right hand find my jawline and then my mouth. He presses them against my lips and my jaw loosens for him, letting him move between my teeth and on to my tongue. His other hand finds my throat, as his hardness presses against me. We haven't had sex in a year. Matthew has barely been able to touch me.

Now, he is knuckles deep in my mouth, his fingertips grazing the back of my throat. When I gag, he pulls back. His other hand leaves my throat, and he yanks my underwear down in one sharp movement, shifting himself so that he is pressed behind me. It occurs to me that in the darkness, I could be anyone. But then so could he.

I feel him adjusting himself with his hand, then he presses into me roughly. The initial shock of pain takes my breath away, and then a hand returns to my throat, squeezing slightly as he builds a rhythm in and out of me. I press a hand against the corner of the bedside table, steadying myself against the force of his... what? I can't find the right word for it. This isn't desire; it feels more like a punishment. And I don't try to stop him, because I deserve it.

His free hand moves to my head, his fingers twisting my hair and pulling it back; his other hand is still clamped around my neck. Matthew grunts as he comes, his body shuddering against mine. He releases me from his hold, and I swallow the air like water, gulping it down thirstily. I sense him roll on to his back, his breathing heavy. His hand returns to my shoulder, where it had started. Neither of us says anything, and as we lie silently in the darkness, I wonder what he's thinking in this moment. I've never known him like that, so intense and forceful.

I wait for him to speak to me, but he doesn't.

He doesn't say it, but I know he blames me. I felt his anger there for the first time, pent up and withheld for all these months. I wonder whether he's spoken to Jess over this past year about the way he really feels towards me. And then a second, worse thought comes to mind – that he may have confided in Reka.

I wonder whether he's like this with her, if she encourages this kind of sex. Maybe that's what he's used to now. What he's come to expect. Another thought follows, uglier than its predecessor. That he's nothing like this with her. That he is gentle and tender. That he makes love to her in the way he used to with me, before we became what we are now.

After a while, his hand slips from my shoulder and I hear the change in Matthew's breathing that tells me he's drifted back into sleep. A part of me resents him this peace, that he can fall so seemingly carelessly into the kind of rest my body craves and hasn't known since before my first pregnancy. Unless he hides it from me, his sleep is safe from the kind of nightmares that scar mine. It doesn't seem fair, yet I know I deserve it.

I turn over and lie on my side with my head rested on my arm. As my eyes adjust to the darkness, I look at Matthew, lying beside me like a stranger in the bed. I wait for sleep to arrive, but like most nights, it fails to come. Instead, I lie silent in the darkness, wondering about the true extent to which my husband hates me.

THIRTEEN

TUESDAY

The following morning, Matthew is up and out of bed before I wake. I hear him downstairs getting ready for work, and I consider staying here until after he's left, so that I won't have to face him. I had lain awake for hours after we'd had sex, eventually pulled into exhausted oblivion. The more I thought of what had happened, the more out of character for Matthew it had seemed.

I get up and put on my dressing gown, realising I can only avoid my husband for so long. When I get to the kitchen, he's at the coffee machine pouring milk into the travel mug he often takes with him to work. There's an awkward silence until he eventually breaks it.

'Does the nursery know Noah won't be in today?'

'I messaged them last night.'

The room falls into silence again.

'Where's Reka?' he asks.

The mention of her name stings my ears.

'I don't know.'

'She isn't in her room. Did you speak to her last night? It

took so long to get Noah to sleep, I think she'd gone to bed by the time I left his room.'

'I haven't seen her to speak to her yet.'

'You'll do it today though?'

He screws the lid on his travel cup before looking at me questioningly.

'Yes,' I say. 'I'll tell her she needs to leave.' Though I wonder whether she might have already gone. She had time yesterday while Matthew was out at work and I was at the hospital with Noah to pack up her things and leave without having to face either of us about what happened.

Matthew holds my gaze, but there's more behind his eyes than the sparse words he has spoken. No matter how stoic Matthew presents himself at times, his eyes always give him away. He comes over to me and kisses my forehead. It's such a gentle gesture after last night's unexpectedly rough sex that it takes me by surprise, and Matthew notices when I recoil from his touch, seemingly slighted by my reaction.

'Are we okay?' he says. 'After—'

'We're fine,' I answer abruptly. I want to ask him why he needs to work late at a job that involves such early starts, but I say nothing. He'll only tell me the same things he's said before: staff meetings, site visits, embellishments on the truth. Excuses, because he can't bear to be in the same room as me for longer than is necessary.

'Your medication,' he says, gesturing to the worktop near the microwave, where he's left my boxes of pills. 'Don't forget, will you?' He can barely bring himself to make eye contact with me. 'I might see you tonight. I'll probably be back late.'

After I hear his car leave the driveway, I make myself a coffee and take it into the conservatory, where I sit alone until I hear Noah's little footsteps padding down the stairs. I go into the hallway to greet him. He looks so small in his Spider-Man pyjamas; so vulnerable with his head still bandaged from yesterday's injury. When he pads past me into the kitchen, I follow. He sits down but I keep my distance. Sometimes, when I sit too closely to him, I sense him flinching from me, my presence seeming to unsettle him. I don't want to hurt him any more than he already is, so I stay at arm's length. It is less painful this way, for both of us.

He reaches for the pens and paper still there from yesterday, and while he draws, I prepare his breakfast. When I take over a bowl of cereal and a plate of sliced fruit, Noah is sitting with his left arm over his picture, keeping it half concealed.

'What are you drawing?' I ask him, knowing he won't answer my question. He may not even allow me to see what he's drawn once he's finished. He is private in so many ways, keeping his thoughts and feelings to himself, locked in a box like a stolen stash of rare jewels he knows shouldn't be in his possession.

I make myself another coffee while he eats. When I take it to sit opposite him, I ask him if I'm allowed to see what he's working on.

He looks at his cereal bowl like a fortune teller studying a crystal ball, as though the answer might be sought from the dribble of milk left in the bottom.

'It's okay,' I tell him. 'You don't have to tell me. Maybe we could wait until you've finished and then you could show me, what do you think? If you'd like to.'

Noah's mouth opens, and I feel a surge of anticipation rise in my chest. I wait for him to say something... and then there is nothing. His mouth closes and he shuts off inside himself again.

My phone starts ringing on the other side of the kitchen, vibrating on the worktop. I get up to see who it is. Jess.

'Jess. How are you?'

'How are you, more importantly? I wanted to check you're okay.'

'I'm okay. Noah not so much, though.' I leave the kitchen

and go into the hallway to tell her about the accident yesterday. 'It looked worse than it was. There was a lot of blood... sent me into a bit of a panic.'

'Understandably. And Reka... I just can't believe she left him like that. You're at home, I'm guessing? Do you think a visit from his favourite honorary auntie might cheer Noah up a bit?'

I manage a smile. 'He would love that.'

'Shall I come over after he's had his lunch? About one thirty?'

'That would be perfect. Thank you.'

I'll need to tidy up before she gets here. My first thought is that the house is a tip, although I'm not sure why it's in such a state. It's not even Noah's things: he rarely plays, and when he does, he does so methodically and deliberately, never pulling out more than his two hands can manage. It would be a comfort to see him immersed in his toys, to have their colour light up these gloom-filled rooms, and yet it seems that even at his tender age, Noah senses the possible dangers presented by a lack of order and self-restraint.

'I'll bring lunch for us, okay, so don't worry about making anything for yourself.'

'You don't need to do that,' I tell her.

'I'd like to. Let me help you.'

You already help so much more than you realise, I think, but I don't say it. As soon as she's said goodbye and the call has ended, I wonder why I didn't.

When I go back into the kitchen, Noah has left the table and is standing at the wooden play kitchen in the corner, transferring plastic pieces of fruit from a shopping basket to a saucepan. I head towards the end of the breakfast bar, where I left the coffee that is probably now cold, but as I pass the table, my attention is drawn to the picture Noah has left half completed, his collection of coloured pens lined up beside it.

There's a fluffy tree drawn in the shape of a green cloud, a single brown line representing the trunk. At the base of the tree, lying on the ground, is a doll-like figure, stick arms and legs poking from its torso at awkward angles, as though it has just fallen a great height from the branches. Scribbled in red is a circle of blood, just behind the doll's head.

'Noah,' I say, trying to keep my voice steady. 'Who's this?'

It might be him, I try to convince myself. This is Noah at the foot of the climbing frame, only he's drawn a tree instead, his memory of the accident altered by the pain he suffered following his injury.

But it is not him. The figure is a girl, with crudely scrawled hair at the side of her head.

Is this how he thinks of her? When he remembers that day, does he see in the same way I do only agony and despair? I wonder how long he will remember it for. He was only three years old when his sister died, and most people are unable to recall much that happened in their lives before the age of four. I hope that time will fade it, that in the months and years to come, Annabelle as she was that day will be replaced by a baby whose giggles and gurgles are the only memory his mind still clings to. I wish the same might apply to me.

As I take in the details of the drawing, my focus rests on the hair. Annabelle was only nine months old when she died, but her scalp was already thick with dark curls that were light and wispy, like feathers to touch. When I look at the image that Noah has created, I see a different version of Annabelle, one older, as she might have been.

A curve of the tree is damp with spilled milk, its colour faded on the flimsy wet paper. Another splash has diluted the red that lies beneath the stick-doll's head, blurring it into a smudge of pink. The hand that holds the drawing is shaking. I stop seeing the image Noah has created; instead, it is replaced with another. The nightmare of Annabelle limp in Noah's arms plays out in front of me, alive on his drawing, and as though without awaiting instruction from my brain, my hands begin to claw at the image, ripping it into shreds.

I stop seeing what I'm doing because all I see is red. The red of her blood. The red of his blood. The red smudge faded to pink on the paper.

My heart is pounding by the time the drawing no longer exists. There are scraps of paper on the breakfast bar and on the floor at my feet. A wave of noise fills my head, ringing in my ears, and it's now I remember Noah is still in the room with me. When I look at him, his eyes meet mine. I realise I can't remember the last time he looked at me as though he was seeing me, our eyes fixed on one another's for this prolonged a length of time. He is crying silently, his face wet with tears, his little jaw set with a smaller, more innocent version of his father's stoicism.

I open my mouth to say something to him, to apologise, to ask his forgiveness. But no sound leaves me. His face red and tear-streaked, Noah flees from the kitchen.

FOURTEEN

TUESDAY

While Noah watches television, I clean the ground floor of the house. As much as I know she is trying to help me, I know Jess doesn't think me able to cope. And she and Matthew talk, possibly far more frequently than I'm aware of. When I see her today, I want her to see a different version of me. One more capable. More in control. Like someone I used to be. Or someone I used to want to be, at least.

I remind myself that today she is not coming here for me. For a while after Annabelle's death, Noah saw a child psychologist. He refused to speak to her, and Matthew and I came to suspect that we were pushing him too soon by trying to make him open up about feelings he was too young to understand. If I wasn't ready to talk about what had happened, how could I expect Noah to be prepared for what it might bring?

Jess has offered several times to try to get him to speak to her, and Matthew and I have allowed her to do so, each time under the guise that she has come over to play. Although only four years old, I think Noah sees through the pretence. Either that, or he has become mistrusting of everyone.

I've got the vacuum cleaner on in the hallway when I hear

music coming from upstairs. It starts as a dull beat through the ceiling, and I ignore it, continuing my chores while trying to shut the sound from my brain. It quickly grows louder. I turn the vacuum cleaner off to be met with the sound of a thumping bass. *She's doing it to wind me up*, I tell myself. I'm not going to let her win.

Every time I've tried to speak to Reka since yesterday afternoon, she hasn't been here. She must be spending her time listening out for what's going on in the rest of the house, timing her departures when she's known I'm distracted. She stayed out long into the evening, avoiding us all. I've sent her texts telling her we need to talk, but they've all gone unanswered. She must realise we want her gone from the house after what happened with Noah, though there's a part of me that sympathises with her. Perhaps she has nowhere to go.

I put the vacuum cleaner back on and finish the hallway before moving into the living room. The bass thunders down the staircase, taunting me, but I grit my teeth and try to tune out the sound, focusing instead on the angry whirr of the vacuum cleaner. I go to the second reception room and then the kitchen, where I instruct Alexa to play Rage Against the Machine. When the first track starts, I tell her to play it louder. The draining board is filthy. I've never realised before just how filthy it is. I clean it every day, despite having a dishwasher. Everything needs to be rinsed off first, and I've always wondered just how much time the machine saves when it requires this preparation.

The bass from upstairs is making the whole house shake.

'Alexa... louder.'

I won't give in to her. Not today. She needs to go, but I can't tell her now, not while she's playing this game with me.

I grab the sponge from the sink and squirt some washing-up liquid on to it. Then I spray down the draining board with surface cleaner and begin to work away at it, scrubbing into the grooves to erase the grime that has become embedded there. I start to feel dizzy, the smell of the cleaning products making me light-headed. And still she taunts me with her presence, the repetitive beat repeated on an endless loop.

'Alexa... louder.'

I move from the draining board to the fridge, where I pull out the fruit and vegetable tray. I empty its contents on to the breakfast bar, leaving the couple of carrots that roll off on to the tiled floor. Like everything else, the fridge is filthy. I feel ashamed at having let things get into such a state. I pull out tubs and packets and bags and bottles, and I line everything up on the breakfast bar in the same way Noah lined up his coloured pens here earlier this morning, because order among the small things sometimes makes the bigger things seem more manage-able, a deception to one's own brain that in maintaining control over a single detail of life, a pattern may form that might affect all others.

I need to go and speak to her, but I can't do it now, not while she's in this mood, trying to taunt me like this. I spray the inside of the empty fridge with disinfectant before taking a cloth to it. The lemon scent hits me in the nose, too strong and overpower-ing. It makes my earlier light-headedness even more potent.

Shut up, I think, trying to force the sound of the bass from my brain. *Shut up, shut up, shut up.*

I hit my head on the side of the fridge as a hand rests on my shoulder.

'Shit! I'm sorry... are you okay?'

Jess's voice wades its way towards me through the cacophony of sounds that fills the room. As my mind tunes back into the noise, I realise Rage Against the Machine remain adamant they can't be told what to do, the washing machine in the utility room is rumbling towards its end with the energy of a rocket set for launch, the food mixer in the corner is turned on without anything in its bowl – a repetitive clunking of metal against metal as it turns in a pointless spin – and the alarm on my phone is going off. Jess has to shout to make herself heard above the racket.

She goes to the freezer, silencing my phone as she passes it.

'Alexa... turn the music off.'

She pulls open the top tray and takes out an ice block, which she wraps in the tea towel that hangs from the oven handle. She passes it to me before turning off the food mixer.

'Do you want to talk about it?'

I act as though I don't know what she means. Then I realise the music from upstairs has stopped. Reka must have heard Jess arrive at the house. Now I look as though I'm the noisy one.

'I know you said you'd bring food, but I was planning on making some soup this afternoon,' I say, gesturing to the contents of the fridge that are lined up on the breakfast bar. 'I've got loads of veg that needs using, and I thought—'

'Suzanna,' Jess says. She points to a brown paper bag near the kettle. 'I've brought food. Shall I make us a cup of tea?'

She goes to the kettle before I offer a response, and as she pulls two mugs from the cupboard, I set about returning the food to the fridge. It looks spotless, but I think now that it might have been clean already. I'm not sure I can remember.

'I thought you were coming later,' I say. 'You said one thirty. I mean, it's no problem, I don't mind you coming here, I just wondered whether something had happened.'

I watch her drop a teabag in each of the mugs. She glances over her shoulder with a knowing look that tells me *I'm* the something that happened. I take the milk from the worktop and pass it to her.

'Is this yours?' Jess holds out her palm to me. She's holding a thin, silver chain-link bracelet.

'No. It's Reka's.' I've seen her wear it often since she first came to live with us. I asked her once where she'd got it from, and she told me it was a gift from her parents after passing her final exams at school. 'Where did you find it?'

'It was by the sugar pot,' Jess says, letting the bracelet slip into my hand. 'Is she here?'

'No,' I say, and I'm not sure why I do. I get the impression Jess has been talking to Matthew. He's probably told her what happened yesterday, how Reka left Noah alone after he'd fallen from the climbing frame. I just hope now that Reka won't come downstairs while Jess is here, although I doubt that'll happen; she hasn't shown her face since the accident. More likely, she'll continue to hide away, especially if she knows Jess is here.

'It's broken,' I say, looking at the snapped chain in my palm.

'Maybe she meant to throw it out. Doesn't look like it can be fixed.'

Jess takes the tea to the dining table, and I settle into a chair opposite her. 'Did something happen this morning?' she asks.

'Matthew called you.'

'Is that a question?'

'No.'

'Suzanna, you're my best friend. And you know that whatever you say to me goes no further. You're a client now as well, which means I have a professional obligation to you, not just a moral duty. I wouldn't jeopardise my career like that. Or our friendship.'

'What's he said to you?'

There's a pause that lasts a little too long. 'Nothing.'

'Jess.'

'He loves you, Suzanna. That's all.'

I sip my tea and avoid making eye contact with her. 'He wants me to tell Reka to go. After yesterday. What happened with Noah.'

'He's told you this?'

'Yesterday, after the accident.'

She watches me with a look of sympathy, and I feel myself grow uncomfortable beneath its heat.

'You're feeling guilty?' she says.

I nod.

'For having to tell Reka to leave, or for what happened to Noah?'

Her words sting.

'It wasn't your fault,' Jess adds. 'Noah was in Reka's care.'

'But I'm his mother.'

'And Matthew is his father.'

My fingers tighten around the mug. 'What do you mean?'

'Well... Matthew wasn't there for him either. Because Noah was in Reka's care. Is he to blame for what happened as well?'

'He wasn't home. I was.'

Jess sips her tea and glances around the spotlessly clean kitchen. 'I think we should have an extra session this week. Tomorrow, if it's convenient for you. I'd like to try the method I've mentioned before.'

I nod. I can't bring myself to agree out loud because it's always sounded such an abhorrent suggestion. The mere thought of it is something I've not been able to contemplate. A part of me wondered whether Jess was mocking me in some way, trying to drag out my misery by proposing such an idea. Yet the more I've thought about it since, the more it's started to make sense. It will be painful and raw. It will force me to confront what I know I've been holding back for all these months.

'I think the time's right,' she says.

'Me too.' Because this is what I'm supposed to say. The truth is I'll never be ready, so I suppose now is as good a time as any.

FIFTEEN
TUESDAY

Jess offers to take Noah to the park for an hour to give him some fresh air and exercise. I'm too exhausted to object. Once they've gone, I go upstairs. I need to talk to Reka, and I've been putting it off now for almost twenty-four hours. The music she played so loudly earlier has been turned off, only silence coming from her bedroom as I stand outside her door. She can't stay inside there for ever, though I don't know where else she would go. She hasn't had much opportunity to form any kind of social circle since moving to the UK, and with our home as remote as it is, the surrounding areas offer little in the way of nightlife or the chance to make friends. I wonder how long she had planned to stay here. She's a young woman with her whole life ahead of her; she must have plans that involve her own dreams and aspirations, perhaps one day a family of her own.

The thought sends a sadness shivering through me. I tap at the door gently and then, when I get no response, I knock again, louder this time.

She can't be in the shower; I would hear the water running. 'Reka.'

I wait politely, respecting her personal space. But then I

remember what happened. Noah's little body on the ground, left alone with his injury to fend for himself. Maybe Matthew's reaction wasn't so over the top after all.

'Reka!'

This is our home, mine and Matthew's and Noah's. I try the door handle. It's locked.

'Reka, you can't avoid us for ever,' I say, trying to keep the tremble from my voice. 'You need to pack your things. It's Matthew's decision,' I add, taking the coward's way out.

'I've got your bracelet,' I tell her. 'You left it in the kitchen. I can find somewhere that's able to fix it for you, if you like?'

I wait a moment longer, feeling my frustration grow with every silent second that passes. We've been good to her. We accepted her as a part of our family, welcoming her into our home at a time when being sociable was the last thing either of us felt ourselves capable of. We've paid her far more than she would have made elsewhere. Yes, we needed her. But I think she grew to need us too. I know she misses her family, and perhaps we offered her the kind of stability she felt she'd lost. Us. The most unstable example of a family anyone might find.

'Reka, I'm sorry,' I say, changing tack. Maybe a heavy-handed approach isn't the way to deal with this. She probably already feels terrible for what happened to Noah, and her avoidance of us all is evidence of her shame. She reacted in panic yesterday, making a split-second decision that turned out to be the wrong one. Haven't we all been guilty of doing the same at least once in our lives?

'I think I understand,' I tell her through the closed door. 'After what happened to Annabelle... you panicked. You were scared how we'd react. I get it, I do. But leaving Noah like that... it should never have happened. I've got to respect Matthew's wishes. I'll do what I can to help you find new employment and somewhere else to live. You won't be thrown out on the streets.'

I don't think Matthew would mind me using him as an excuse. He knows I hate any kind of conflict or confrontation. And I understand why he feels Reka needs to go. I just wish that what happened yesterday could be undone somehow. I can't imagine Noah taking to another nanny the way he has to Reka. We will never be lucky enough to have it so easy a second time around. I wish there wasn't the need for us to have one at all, but I know I still can't bring myself to be the mother he deserves.

'Please have your things packed before Matthew comes home tonight. I'll drive you to a hotel... I'm happy to pay for it. I just don't want this to be made harder for anyone than it already is.'

Still, I get no response. I wonder whether her guilt relates solely to Noah's fall, or if there's more to it. Matthew.

I move away from the door and go to the staircase, where I wait a moment, listening for signs of life. But Reka is quiet, refusing to let her presence be known.

Jess will be back home with Noah soon, and she'll likely want to play with him alone. She tries role play sometimes, using the figures from Noah's *Paw Patrol* set to get him to open up about his feelings. So far, it has yet to work. I've never asked to sit in with them while they're playing like this. My son's perpetual silence is already hard enough to live with, and I fear that with me there, he will only close in on himself more. I think I'm probably the problem, but how is a four-year-old child supposed to articulate that to an adult?

I go downstairs, make myself a coffee and take it into the garden. The spade still rests beneath the beech tree, abandoned there after its last use. The azaleas and camellias I have yet to plant are waiting in their pots, in need of watering. There's time for me to plant them into the ground now, particularly as Jess will be looking after Noah.

Ten minutes into digging, it begins to rain. I hear Jess's car pull up on the driveway, her tyres crunching across the gravel as she pulls to a stop outside the house. I see a flash of Noah's coat in the hallway; moments later, Jess appears at the back doors.

'Azaleas,' she says, making her way across the lawn. 'Beautiful. They'll look lovely there.'

'Where's Noah?'

'He's in the living room. I put the TV on for him so I could come to speak to you... I hope that was okay.'

'Yeah. No problem. I mean, I'm fine. I'll come in now and grab Noah a snack.'

'Suzanna,' Jess says, in that calming tone she always uses during our sessions, 'has something happened?'

'I haven't spoken to Reka yet.'

'About what?'

'Leaving. I mean, I've spoken *to* her, but not *with* her... She won't come out of her room to talk to me. I've been worried about upsetting her, which I know seems ridiculous after what happened yesterday, but it occurred to me that she's all alone over here really and she doesn't have any family or friends to fall back on, and she's always been so good with Noah until what happened with the fall, but I think she was probably scared after everything she knows about Annabelle, and she probably feared how we'd react, even though I know it was just an accident and she made a mistake in leaving him, but we've all made mistakes and done things we regret—'

'Suzanna.' Jess takes me by the arm, her grip tight, keeping me upright. 'It's okay. Everything's going to be okay.'

The rain is ice cold on my skin, running now in rivulets down my bare arms. My weight is pitched forward, resting on the spade. There is soil beneath my fingernails, the acidic odour of it clinging to the air that circles us.

'Let go,' she says softly as she gently prises my fingers from the spade's handle. 'It's okay... you can let it go.'

When I meet her eye, I feel as though I'm looking at a

stranger. It's not just Jess: it's everything around me. The garden no longer looks familiar; the house looms over us like a place I've yet to enter. I feel disconnected from everything around me, plucked from all that is recognisable and lowered into a life that bears resemblances to mine and yet somehow is completely different. Yet perhaps she feels the same. I see in her eyes that she doesn't quite know what to make of me in this moment: my trainers sunk into the soil, my hair matted on my face, my clothing stuck to my skin with rainwater.

'Suzanna,' she says, speaking my name carefully – in therapist mode now, rather than as a friend. 'Is this about Reka?'

I feel my blood run cold. 'What do you mean?'

'This,' she says, gesturing to the upturned ground. 'The frantic digging, the excessive cleaning... the need to organise. Are you feeling upset about her leaving?'

'Of course.'

Jess puts a hand on my arm as she drops the spade from the other. 'The trainers she always wears are still by the front door.'

I feel my jaw tense. 'I've given her until the end of the day.'

Jess's hand slips from my arm. She's still looking at me in that way I can't quite decipher. Like she doesn't quite trust me. And maybe she's right not to. I'm not sure I can trust myself any more.

SIXTEEN

TUESDAY

Matthew gets home that evening while I'm upstairs with Noah, who is in the bath. I wait for him to come upstairs to see us, but he doesn't. I sit on the lid of the toilet seat and watch as Noah moves a plastic boat in circles through the thick foam of bubble bath I poured too generously. His face is impassive, as it usually is, his actions aimless yet deliberate. I wonder what he's thinking. I wonder if even he knows, or whether his mind drifts to places that his child's brain can't yet comprehend.

I wait a while longer, unsure whether I'm hopeful that Matthew might join us. By the time I reach to help Noah from the bath, the water has gone cold. Noah's fingertips have shrivelled like prunes. I wrap a towel around him and tuck it in at his chest, and he follows me to his bedroom. We move silently through the motions of bedtime: put on pyjamas, dry hair, brush teeth. I wonder if Noah recognises the absence of his father from the routine. When I ask him to pick a story, tonight it's a tale about a dragon who likes to play dressing up, a book that he picked at the library when he went there with Reka a couple of weeks ago. I'm sure she vetted his choice of books before she borrowed them each visit, careful to make sure there was nothing in any that might trigger an upsetting memory or an adverse reaction. No stories about families or friendships. Nothing that involves the protagonist being in any kind of peril. And certainly no stories about siblings. It must have limited their choices to a bare minimum.

I'm nearing the last page when Noah speaks to me.

'Is Reka gone?'

My son's voice shouldn't provoke the kind of reaction it does, but I can't help it. It's a rare sound, beautiful and alien; I want to catch it between my hands like a butterfly, to hold it there for a moment and admire its patterns before it flies away from me.

'Did you see her leave?'

But Noah looks at me with those sad, distant eyes and says nothing more. He must have seen her this afternoon, at some time between Jess leaving and teatime. Reka must have waited for a moment to sneak out, still trying to avoid Matthew and me.

I read the last page and pull the duvet up over him. 'Wait here a moment. I'll be back in a second.'

I leave the room and go to the staircase, but I don't need to go downstairs to see confirmation of what Noah has suggested. At the bottom of the stairs on the shoe rack by the front door, the trainers Jess had earlier commented on seeing still there are gone. I wait for a moment, listening for a sound from Matthew. But I don't know where he is, and I don't want him to catch me standing here.

When I return to Noah's bedroom, he has already fallen asleep. I turn off the night light and sit on the carpet beside his bed, looking at his sleeping face shrouded in shadow. He is beautiful. Perfect. But I know that I will damage him, in the way I seem to damage everything.

I hear Matthew's footsteps on the landing. With Noah's breathing deep and peaceful, I get up from the carpet quietly and pull his door not-quite shut, so that the light from the landing can filter through. I go down to our bedroom, expecting to find Matthew there, but he isn't. I hear a noise along the landing, and then I realise that Matthew is in Reka's bedroom.

My heart knocks against my chest, sending a warning signal I don't understand. He isn't *with* her. I haven't heard or seen her all evening, so he can't be. Maybe Noah is right; maybe Reka is gone. A selfish pang of regret bursts in my chest. I should have spoken to her about Matthew again. We should have talked about everything, cleared the air between us. Despite everything, I've needed her. And she was good for Noah. He needed her, maybe more than he's needed me.

When I go down to her room, the door is wide open. Matthew is standing at the side of the bed, facing the window. He hears me enter the room.

'She's left, then.'

I go to stand beside him. The room looks so different to how it did before Reka came here. She decorated, as we'd said she could: the walls a light sage green, voile curtains hanging to the carpet, the bed scattered with cushions and throws. It looks very much like a student's bedroom, adorned with the paraphernalia of youth. Above the chest of drawers, there's a corkboard pinned with photographs and birthday cards, treasures from family back home in Hungary.

'Has she?'

It seems strange to me that these photographs that Reka treasures enough to have brought to the UK with her would be left behind so carelessly – her beloved *anya*, her *apa*, her sister, Celina.

His beautiful brown eyes question me. 'It seems so.'

Does it? I think. There are still clothes at the end of the bed and hair products on the bedside table. A book sits with its spine bent, folded open on the page where she last stopped reading.

'Where's her laptop?' Matthew asks, watching me as I scan

the room, and seeming to read my thoughts. 'Phone charger... that sort of thing?'

He's right: she seems to have taken all the day-to-day items a life now needs. The wardrobe is half empty, though I've no way of knowing how filled with her things it had been anyway. And her trainers have gone. I suspect when I go downstairs, I'll find the pink raincoat she always wore will no longer be hanging on the coat hooks, either.

'You're right,' I say quietly. Reka has left us.

We stand in silence for a moment, and when I look at Matthew, he appears to be lost somewhere in his own thoughts.

'Are you okay?' I ask, but he doesn't seem to hear me. 'Matthew.'

'She's gone,' he says, snapping out of the trance he seemed to have fallen into. 'It's for the best.'

He comes to me and puts his hands on my upper arms. 'Are you okay? You look tired.'

Past his shoulder, I see the crumpled duvet pushed down on the bed and the creased sheet that's coming loose from the mattress at its corner. I see him with her, here in her bedroom, and I hear her voice whispering his name.

'Suzanna.'

Now it's his turn to pull me back to the present, yanking me from the vision of them together.

'Didn't you see her this afternoon?'

I shake my head. 'Jess came over. She took Noah to the park for a couple of hours. Reka must have waited until later to leave.'

Matthew's jaw is set tightly. 'I can't believe she didn't speak to either of us before she left. I didn't have her down as such a coward.'

Is he protesting too much? I wonder if he's angry with her for ending their affair, or if he was the one who ended things, and he resents the way she's just been able to walk away from the situation. I'm not even sure I'm upset with Reka any more. If anything happened between them, then Matthew is to blame. He's the one with the family. He's thirteen years older than Reka, as well as her employer. He took advantage of his position, and now she's been left with no home to go to.

His hands slide up to my shoulders and he squeezes too tightly, his fingers pinching my skin. When he pulls me to his chest, I can hear his heartbeat, its rhythm too fast. His cold lips press against my forehead before moving across my hair, his words spoken softly against my ear.

'I guess it's just us again.'

SEVENTEEN

WEDNESDAY

It rains heavily in the early hours of Wednesday morning. I lie awake for a while, listening to Matthew snore gently beside me as the downpour lashes at the window. I resent his sleep. I resent the peace with which he seems capable of falling into oblivion, and the depth of rest into which he can recharge. He doesn't seem to hurt in the way that I do, from head to toe, diseased by an ache that can't be treated. He isn't plagued by guilt in the way that I am, although he has no reason to be. He wasn't there that day to alter how things might have ended.

But I was.

I get up while Matthew and Noah are still asleep, and I sit in the conservatory, watching the rain assault the lawn and the flower beds that curve around the borders of the garden. Winter seems to have lasted an age. Everything still looks grey and fragile. Dead.

'I wondered where you were.'

I jump at the sound of Matthew's voice. I turn from the window to see him holding two cups of coffee, and when he comes into the conservatory, he passes one to me. I take it gratefully, needing the caffeine, but when I look at him, I no longer feel sure of the person I'm seeing.

'Still here,' I say, but my choice of words throws a strange and unsettled silence over us that leaves me feeling uncomfortable.

'She'll probably come back for the rest of her things today.'

'Why do you think that?' I ask, wondering why he can't even bring himself to speak Reka's name.

'She won't want to leave it until the weekend. She knows I'll be at work... She's probably trying to avoid me.'

Why would she want to avoid you? I think, but I say nothing, knowing that any excuse he'd give would relate to Noah's accident on Monday. There's no reason for Matthew to admit to an affair now, not with Reka gone from our lives.

'You know Jess is coming here this morning?' I ask, changing the subject.

'You didn't say.'

I thought I had, but I must have forgotten. 'She thinks we should try what she spoke about before.'

Matthew raises an eyebrow. 'But what do you think? It doesn't matter what Jess wants.'

'She wants what's best for me.'

'So do I.'

'I know that, I wasn't saying otherwise, I just...' But I don't know how to finish. 'I'm sorry.'

Matthew takes his coffee and heads back into the house. He's angry with me, but I don't know why.

He doesn't speak to me again, leaving for work without saying goodbye. When Noah wakes up, I ask him if he wants to go to nursery today, and he nods. I get him ready and give him breakfast, then I drive him to the school, grateful that he seems happy to go in. Or maybe it's just relief to get away from me.

When I get back home, I watch at the living room window, waiting to see Jess's car. By the time 10 a.m. arrives, I've bitten my thumbnail down to the quick, where the skin stings and turns an angry red. A succession of 'what if' scenarios plays out in my head. 'What if' has been an enemy of mine for as long as I'm able to remember, standing in doorways to stop me passing, whispering in my ear at night to keep me awake. It has been the sibling I never had, competitive and sneaky, tripping me up then feigning innocence when I fall. Now, it stands here beside me, taunting me with everything that could go wrong.

What if it makes things worse?

What if it doesn't work?

What if it makes the nightmares more terrifying?

The rational part of my brain can offer a response to all these doubts: things can't get any worse, I have nothing to lose, the nightmares can't be any more terrifying than they already are. Yet still I let it mock me, let it dare me to call Jess and make up a last-minute excuse for having to cancel this morning's session.

But I don't. I see Jess's car pull on to the driveway and I go to the front door to greet her.

'Are you still ready to talk to her today?' Jess asks as I follow her down the hallway. 'This is entirely your choice, Suzanna – it isn't suitable for everyone, but when it works, it can be incredibly effective as a tool for healing. It's up to you.'

I nod. Until today, I had never believed I could do this. I had never wanted to do it. But I have nothing left to lose. I can feel myself falling apart at the seams, a life coming undone one stitch at a time. I owe it to Noah to save myself before I drag him down with me. I owe it to Matthew, regardless of what he thinks of me.

We go into the second reception room and Jess waits for me to sit before she closes the door. She always does this, even when there's no one but us in the house.

'Try to relax your shoulders,' Jess tells me.

I close my eyes and allow myself to sink back into the sofa.

'Let's do the breathing exercises first. In through the nose for four counts, out through the mouth for eight.'

I follow her lead and count out the numbers in my head, focusing on my breaths to try to stop my mind from wandering too far ahead of itself. After a minute or so, Jess speaks again.

'Are you ready, Suzanna?'

'Yes.'

'Okay. I want you to picture yourself with Annabelle. She is in front of you. Perhaps you are holding her in your arms. Maybe she is lying on a playmat on the floor. Just allow yourself a minute or two to set the scene. Take in the surroundings, observe the details. Then when you're ready, I want you to rest your focus on Annabelle.'

Try as I might, the vision of her won't come. My brain has blocked the ability to picture her, a kind of self-preservation, a dam that holds back the flood that will follow.

'Can you see her?' Jess asks softly, her voice lowered to little more than a whisper.

'No.'

'That's okay. Try to think of a favourite day. Maybe it was Christmas... Maybe a day out you shared together. It doesn't have to be anything special either; it could just be a moment in the house, just the two of you.'

My mind snags on the thought of the first birthday that never was. I had spoken to Matthew about it just weeks before she left us, and he'd responded in his predictable way by saying it was pointless throwing a party for a one-year-old who wouldn't even remember it. But it was special, I'd told him. A milestone. Why shouldn't we celebrate at every possible opportunity, when life is the special occasion?

The truth was that although the idea of celebrating was something I knew we should embrace, I was exhausted. What I'd been hoping for was that Matthew would offer to arrange it all. It didn't need to be anything fancy: a few of Noah's classmates from the nursery, some party games and a cake. I'd just wanted him to say yes, and for him to make the calls or send the texts. I just wanted him to take some pressure off me, but he'd been too distracted by other things.

And then it was too late.

'Visualise your surroundings,' Jess continues. 'Where are you?'

'In her bedroom.'

'Okay. So what does it look like? Think of yourself as though you're holding a camera. Start with the wider picture and then zoom in on the details.'

It is easy enough to see the room. The lemon-yellow walls... the daisy chain border... the soft cotton curtain that hangs around the end of the cot. I see the bookcase beneath the windowsill, stacked with the baby books Annabelle inherited from Noah. The trinkets and ornaments and photo frames lined on top, most of which were gifted from friends and family when she was born. The child's-size wardrobe curved in shape like the furniture from *Beauty and the Beast*. It is all so easy to visualise because it remains exactly as it was on the day she died. Sometimes, I go in there and lie on the carpet, my face rested on one of her soft toys. That fresh-from-the-bath, newborn baby skin scent still lingers there, like I'm able to breathe her in.

'Where is she, Suzanna? Do you see her?'

The first thing my mind throws into the scene is the rocker chair I'd carried down to the living room just hours before my daughter had died.

My mind hates me. I've always known this, and it was never clearer than in those months after Annabelle was born. Like 'what if' interludes, intrusive thoughts have been a sidekick of mine for most of my life, the kind of company you don't want to be around but don't know how to get rid of without drawing negative attention to yourself. In my younger years, it caused me to feel socially awkward, to say the wrong things at inappropriate moments; to have thoughts I could never share with anyone for fear of being regarded as insane. When I met Jess in the halls where we both stayed in our first year at university, we forged an instant bond that made us firm friends from that first meeting, but I never shared with her the extent of my anxieties, fearful that it would scare her away. Even now, after everything, I have yet to be entirely honest with her about the images that plague me.

After Annabelle's birth, the thoughts became increasingly violent. They terrified me. I was scared of my own mind, of myself – a person it was impossible to run away from – and the only person I could confide in was Jess. Any other therapist might have tried to have me sectioned.

'Suzanna, are you okay?'

I shake my head. 'The rocker chair.'

'Let it come,' she advises me, as she has done so many times before. 'Don't try to fight the image off, it'll only get stronger. Allow yourself to see it, to focus on it, and then let it pass through.'

She has offered me this same advice before, during treatment for what she referred to as postnatal depression. *Don't try to fight the image away. See it, know that it isn't real... allow it to come and then let it pass. If you try to block it, the resistance against it will only make its appearance known more strongly.*

Like trying to play dead until an assailant flees the scene.

'Where are you in the room?' Jess asks me.

'On the carpet.'

'And where is Annabelle?'

'Sitting on the rug beside me.'

My chest swells with a sharp intake of breath at the sight of my daughter. She is wearing a spotty Babygro, her chubby little hands balled into fists in her lap. Her long dark lashes flutter as she blinks.

'What would you like to say to her, Suzanna?'

'That I love her. That I'm sorry. That we'll miss her every day for the rest of our lives.'

'So tell her. Now's your chance.'

'Noah misses you. He hasn't found the words to talk about you yet, but I know he does. Maybe one day, when he's a bit older, he'll be able to speak to you and tell you. I heard him singing, just the other day. I think he was singing to you.'

My words freeze. I'm still not sure Noah ever heard me sing that song to Annabelle, and I don't know how he could have heard it from Reka, like he'd said. My memory is failing me, taunting me as it leaves.

'And what about you, Suzanna?' Jess prompts. My eyes are still closed. I am still with Annabelle in her bedroom; Jess has become a bodyless voice directing me.

And now, it is like something has been opened, a cap unscrewed to relieve the pressure.

'I don't know what happened,' I say, speaking to Annabelle. 'Or why it happened. I owe you a reason, but I don't have one. I was so exhausted. It's the worst, most pathetic of excuses. Life felt tilted on its side, like nothing was quite clear or made sense, but I suppose that's how it must be for all parents with a baby and a toddler. We're all just surviving, just making it from one day to the next. So many times I've gone back over that afternoon and played it out differently in my head, just for an alternative outcome. If we'd gone out to the park... If I'd taken you and Noah to soft play... If I'd just asked someone for help. If I'd just said to your dad, "I can't do this today, I need you to let me sleep for an hour." But asking for help felt like failure, and I wanted to be better than I was. I wanted to manage. What is that? Pride? Stupidity? Whatever it was, I failed you in the worst kind of way. It was neglect. It was unforgivable. And regardless of what he thinks now, or the ideas he may have about himself as he grows up, it wasn't Noah's fault. I've considered what it might be like to blame him. I've pictured him lifting you from your rocker chair... I've tried to visualise what might have happened, all the while fighting that very scene from playing out in my head. I wondered whether I could absolve myself of responsibility somehow, just to give myself a few moments respite from the guilt. What sort of mother does that make me... what sort of person? I'm the adult. I'm the parent. I should have protected you and I didn't. You should be here now, running rings around your dad and me, but you're not, and I know he will never forgive me. He wears the right face, and he speaks the right words, but I see it in his eyes when he looks at me. Every time he looks at me, he sees what I did. What I didn't do. How does anyone even begin to get beyond that?'

I feel a hand on my shoulder and my eyes snap open. It's only now I realise I've been clawing at my hands, a short, jagged slice of thumbnail cutting repeatedly into my palm, drawing blood. I expect to find Jess beside me, but she is still sitting in the chair opposite, her face impassive as she watches me. And for the first time during one of these sessions, I am crying.

EIGHTEEN
WEDNESDAY

Upstairs in the bathroom, I use a make-up removal wipe to clean off the smudged mascara around my eyes. Jess has gone to collect Noah from nursery, refusing to let me do so in the state I got myself into. When I look in the mirror, I barely recognise myself. I am a physical embodiment of the effects Jess had warned me this approach to my therapy would take, exhausted and depleted. Months ago, she had told me to think of myself as a bottle of lemonade, as yet unopened. She talked about pressure, and with each little twist of the cap, a little being released, session by session. 'What happens if you twist that cap straight off in one go?' she'd asked me. 'It's messy. It's going to take a bit of clearing up.'

By the time I hear her car pulling up on the gravel driveway, I'm almost presentable. I run my fingertips under my eyes, wiping away any last sign of tears. The last thing I want is for Noah to see me upset.

'You need to rest now,' Jess says, putting a hand on my arm after Noah has gone into the living room. 'This morning was traumatic for you. But I do believe it'll help, in the long term.'

'Is Noah okay?'

'He's fine. It's you who's not. Look, I'm going to have to head off to work, but are you able to get some rest this afternoon? What time will Matthew be home?'

'I'm not sure. But it'll be okay... Noah and I will have a quiet afternoon.'

I say it as though there's anything other for him, and the guilt is overwhelming. I know I need to do better, but I just can't bring myself to. I am so exhausted all the time.

Jess leaves, and when I go into the living room, Noah is playing with his *Paw Patrol* figures. I sit at the end of the sofa and curl my legs beneath me, feeling my eyelids pulling with the weight of tiredness.

It takes me back there, to that day.

My God, I'd been so tired. Annabelle still wasn't sleeping for more than a couple of hours at a time, and Noah had been going through a phase of having nightmares. He would often wake up crying and sweat-soaked, and I would lie beside him in the darkness, trying to soothe him back to sleep while his sister suckled on a breast at my other side. For months I had been a zombie moving through our house, existing but never truly present. I'd felt my life altered beyond all recognition, and I'd stopped believing that anything would ever be any different to the constant exhaustion and feeling of failure that I wore like a second skin.

That day, I'd been especially tired. All morning, I had done little, just about managing to deal with the most basic tasks of loading the dishwasher and preparing Noah's breakfast. Matthew had left early for work, before 5 a.m. I'd let Noah watch far more television than he would usually have been allowed, but I didn't have the energy to feel guilty about it.

I managed to make lunch for Noah, I remember that. Pasta and cheese, which I'd found two days later, half eaten and dried up, still on a plastic plate on the stove of the wooden play kitchen where I'd allowed him to sit to eat. I'd washed the saucepan, with little needing to be cleared up. There was something on the television in the living room: something noisy and colourful, with annoying songs. Its light and life filled the room where I couldn't. After he'd eaten, I took the children in there and closed the door so that Noah couldn't wander around the house. I was so tired. I asked him to cuddle up with Annabelle and me on the sofa, and when she fell asleep on my breast, I moved her into the rocker chair that was sitting at the side of the coffee table. Noah sat beside me and watched the television. I was aware of having to fight to keep my eyes open, and at some point, I went to the kitchen to get a glass of water. I'm not sure when it was knocked to the floor, but I noticed it there later, the edge of the glass chipped, and the water soaked through the corner of the rug.

The first thing I remember from when I woke up was the song that was blaring from the television. My hearing was more acute than my vision, with my eyes still fighting to gain clarity. When it cleared, Noah was standing at the side of the sofa, holding Annabelle in his arms.

It took seconds to realise what had happened, for me to register the fact that I had fallen asleep while my children were in my care. I had no idea what the time was, no idea of how long I might have been sleeping. When I sat up, my head swayed with a weight of sickness, like a hangover without the aid of alcohol. There was sick on Annabelle's Babygro, white milky lumps staining the floral pattern across her chest. I saw this, and then I registered the look on Noah's face, and I wondered why he looked so frightened, that I might tell him off for Annabelle's sickness.

She wasn't moving. The realisation of the fact didn't creep up on me in stages; more, it floored me like a blow to the face, a single knock-out punch that sent me reeling. Noah was clutching her to his chest, like a doll. He was squeezing her too hard. I said something to him, but later, I couldn't remember what it had been.

I might have grabbed her from him. I might have coaxed him gently to hand her to me, but I don't recall what happened in those moments that followed: that slightest slice of time that preceded the end of our life as we had known it. All I'm certain of is that when I took her from her brother, I felt the lifelessness of my baby in my hands, my heart struck by the pain of the truth before my brain could be sure of it. She looked asleep: her eyes closed, her rosebud lips parted ever so slightly, her thick hair curled at her ears. But when I looked at her face for longer, I could see the colour gone, the greyness that had sunk within her skin and embedded itself there as permanent. I looked at Noah, registered his fear for a second time, this time reading it so differently to the first, and then I screamed, though I didn't hear the sound until much later, in the weeks and months that followed.

At some point, I realised that Noah was no longer there. I sat on the sofa with Annabelle held to my chest, rocking her back and forth as though if I could simply love her enough, I could bring her back to life.

Three days later, after a post-mortem, we were told that a single blow to the head from being dropped had caused a fatal fracture to the base of Annabelle's skull. My beautiful daughter was dead, and my son now bore the burden, forever changed by what had happened that afternoon. I was guilty of killing them both.

NINETEEN

WEDNESDAY

Later that afternoon, after Matthew has arrived home from work, I prepare dinner for this evening while he goes out for a run. I hear footsteps on the landing. It isn't Noah: he's in the living room where I left him, building a Duplo fortress to house his collection of plastic zoo animals, and I know it's not him because the footsteps are too heavy. Matthew had said that Reka would return, and now it occurs to me that she must have waited out the front somewhere to see him leave for a run before she came into the house to collect the rest of her things.

If I'm able to avoid her, it might be for the best. I don't have the energy for a confrontation, and I don't want to make things any harder for her than they already are. Noah is safe now, and that's all that matters. If anything did happen between Reka and Matthew, I'm not sure I feel any resentment towards her for it. It's all complicated. She was innocent when she arrived here, and we should never have dragged her into the tragedy of our family.

I continue to peel potatoes, throwing them absent-mindedly into the saucepan of water that rests on the cooker top. From upstairs, I hear drawers and cupboards being opened and closed, and a short time later, while I'm frying off onions, I hear the footsteps head back down the stairs. My breath catches in my throat because I know she's going to come to find me before she leaves. And right on cue, the kitchen door falls open, and I am no longer alone with my thoughts.

'You're leaving,' I say: a statement rather than a question.

But she says nothing, continuing to punish me with the silent treatment.

'If you need a reference, I'll provide one for you. You've been good to us. Noah lo—' I cut myself short, finding the truth too painful to admit.

I put down the knife and close my eyes, trying to regulate my heart rate by breathing more slowly.

'Reka... I need to apologise. I know I haven't been the easiest person to live with. The truth is...' But I can't get it out. I stand with my hands pressed to the kitchen worktop and take a deep breath. 'You know that I thought there might have been something going on between you and Matthew,' I blurt before I allow myself time to change my mind. 'I realise now how foolish that was. He isn't that kind of man. And I don't think you're that kind of woman, either... I know we've not known each other very long, but I know you're a good person, Reka, and I'm sorry if I've treated you unkindly. I haven't been myself recently. I haven't been myself since Annabelle... you know. Sometimes, I think that woman is gone. She must be, mustn't she, because how can anyone return to a version of themselves that they were before something like that happened? Jess calls it traumatic grief. She uses the word grief a lot. Trauma. I don't think it's even that. I feel emptied, like everything that was once a part of who I was has been tipped up and shaken out of me, and now I'm just arteries and veins and organs, the blood still pumping but the life gone. I thought I was going to lose Noah. I got it into my head that you and Matthew were plotting to take him away from me. It makes sense in a way that I might worry about losing him, doesn't it, because I haven't been a good mother to him... I haven't been any kind of mother. I'm just a woman who lives in the same house as him. A ghost, really. I haven't been able to touch him. Some days I can barely bring myself to look at him. And yet the thought of losing him is like a second death. I know it was ridiculous. I know you've just been trying to help me. And if anything's gone on with Matthew... it isn't you... it's me. I'm not myself, you see. I don't know how to feel any more... how to function like a normal person.'

When I stop talking, I realise I've gone light-headed. There are lights in front of my eyes, flashing silver streaks, and the tinnitus in my ears is shrill and persistent.

You're going to have to say something.

I turn sharply at the sound of her voice. 'What was that?'

You're going to have to tell someone what you did.

I see her smile at me, dead-eyed and unfeeling, and a memory resurfaces, my hands beneath her arms, dragging her up from the hallway floor.

A sound from outside the kitchen snatches my attention. Noah appears at the doorway, clutching his toy beagle to his chest, its cuddle-worn ears hanging limp at the sides of its head.

'Mummy,' he says, looking at me with furrowed eyebrows, 'who are you talking to?'

PART TWO

MATTHEW

TWENTY

WEDNESDAY

I hear Noah calling for me before I reach the driveway. The front door is wide open, but I know I clicked it shut on my way out. I pick up my pace and race up the driveway, reaching the hallway to find Noah on the staircase, standing there with his trainers on. They are caked in mud. He's already been upstairs and come back down: there's a trail of mud tracking his path.

'Hey, mate,' I say, holding out sweat-slicked arms, though I know he won't accept them. 'Were you looking for me?'

He comes down the last few steps, but he doesn't accept the offer of a hug. Sometimes he will, mostly he won't. I never try to push it. Instead, he stands looking at me wide-eyed, with the expression of displacement he wears now as a second skin.

'Has something happened?'

I glance back at the open front door, thinking how easy it would have been for Noah to just walk out of the house. He could have ended up on one of the lanes, lost and alone. An image flashes into my head: Suzanna on the sofa, cradling Annabelle; our daughter's tiny face smothered from sight. I close my eyes for a second, trying to push the memory away.

'Where's your mum?'

'Garden.' Noah's voice comes small and tentative.

I gesture to the mud on his shoes. 'You been helping?' I ask with a laugh, trying to conceal the concern that has settled in my gut. I just want to see him smile. Just once, if only briefly. I just want everything to feel for once the way it did before, back when we were happy. People say it will come, in time. But they don't know. No one knows. I don't see a way in which any of us could ever be happy again. Even if it was possible, the guilt of living our lives while our daughter is gone would be too much to bear.

'What's she doing?' I ask.

'Digging.'

I'd known Suzanna would struggle after her session with Jess this morning. I didn't want her to go through with it, but it's not my choice to make. I swallow the lump of resentment that builds in my throat. I know Suzanna is probably dissecting every moment of that ninety minutes with the scrutiny of a pathologist carrying out a post-mortem. No detail will be ignored. No single word will be left unanalysed. She'll pick it all apart and put it back together again in a hundred different ways, to see if she can alter the reality of it. Then she'll find herself back at the start and do it all again, the digging a useless attempt at distraction while she tortures herself over and over.

For a while, I believed she deserved it.

'She's gone,' Noah says flatly.

My heart cracks for him. It wasn't his fault. He's just a child.

I crouch in front of him. 'But she's never really gone,' I tell him, and I press two fingertips to the left of his chest. 'She's always in here,' I say, before moving my fingers to his forehead. 'And in here. Would you like to go and play with some of her toys?'

This is what we've been advised to encourage. Immersing Noah among Annabelle's things will apparently make him more comfortable with the idea of talking about her, though we've been warned it may take time.

His light-haired eyebrows knit together, and he turns to glance down the hallway towards the kitchen. When he looks back, he can't make eye contact with me. He tightens his grip on Benji, and I realise with a sinking feeling in my chest that he's not talking about Annabelle.

'Who's gone?' I put a hand on his shoulder. 'Noah. Who's gone?'

He looks on the verge of tears.

'I'm sorry, mate.' I squeeze his shoulder and stand, moving away and giving him space. 'You're okay. Don't worry about anything.'

When I head towards the kitchen, it's like I'm being pulled there by a magnetic force that's so much stronger than I am. The back doors leading out on to the patio are open. Some of Noah's toys are strewn on the slabs: a set of plastic skittles, a football, a mini golf set. His balance bike is propped against the table.

At the far end of the garden, beneath the beech tree, Suzanna is hunched over a spade, her feet sunk in the soft earth of one of the flower beds. She looks older in a way I've never seen her, fatigued and defeated. Yet when she begins to move, she does so with a determined rhythm, back and forth, back and forth, turning mound after mound of earth.

'Suzanna.'

She doesn't hear me. I check behind me for Noah, who has sat down at the kitchen table, not wanting to come back outside. When I go down to the bottom of the garden, I say her name again, but she still doesn't hear me. Either that or she chooses to ignore me.

It's now that I see the strip of floral fabric. When Reka had first come here, I'd made a comment to Suzanna about how she always wore one of those headbands with a knot at the top –

how they gave her the look of a dungaree-wearing 1940s propaganda poster girl. It had almost raised a smile from my wife, but not quite.

I realise now I haven't seen Reka all week. It's not unusual for me to go days without seeing her: I often leave early for work before the rest of the house is up and functioning, and in the evenings, she makes herself scarce to give us family time. She occasionally joins us at weekends, but mostly she allows us the time we need to try to rebuild. Though she'd been asked to leave after Noah's accident, neither Suzanna nor I had thought she'd left. Not until last night, at least.

I can taste bile in the back of my throat.

'Suzanna... what are you doing?'

The spade edge slices into the ground and Suzanna looks up from her task. She pushes her hair back from her face with her arm, and when she looks at me, I can see the smeared mascara that runs from her eyes in black rivulets. Her cheeks are red and flushed. She looks at me and through me, seemingly unaware that I'm standing right in front of her.

I glance at Reka's headband on the ground, its pink and green pattern stained with mud.

'Suzanna,' I say, 'where's Reka?'

TWENTY-ONE
WEDNESDAY

The call to Jess connects, but I can barely keep my voice steady. I don't want to be making this call: not to her, not to anyone.

But I can't let Noah be exposed to what I now fear might come next.

'Any chance you can come over? I'm sorry... I'm desperate.'

'What's happened?' she asks.

'Nothing,' I answer, a little too quickly. 'I mean, it's fine. I just... Could you take Noah to the park for me or something? Just get him away from the house for a bit?'

I wish there was someone else I could call, but there isn't. Suzanna's parents both died years ago, and my mother is confined to a nursing home, her memory of who I am now a gift imparted to me on special occasions. When we'd moved to this place, we'd intended to form a social circle, though it had been much more difficult than we'd anticipated. And then Annabelle died, and we shut ourselves off from everything.

'The park? It's forecast to pour down.' Jess falls quiet for a moment. I imagine her contemplating what the hell might be going on here. But she could never imagine this. 'Is Suzanna okay? Has she done something?'

Nothing you're assuming, I think because Jess's first thoughts seem to be that Suzanna has done something to hurt herself. She is so vulnerable, and regardless of her sessions with Jess, neither of us really knows the extent of what's going on inside her head. But if one of us did, perhaps we wouldn't have found ourselves here.

'I don't know.'

'I'm leaving now,' Jess tells me, and I hang up wondering whether I've done the right thing. I go back into the kitchen and look out through the doors. Suzanna has stopped digging. She is sitting on the overturned soil, her palms flat beside her on the damp earth.

'Noah,' I say, searching the cupboards for the water bottle he takes with him to nursery. 'Auntie Jess is going to take you to the park for a bit, okay?' Sickness somersaults in my stomach as I speak the words.

He says nothing as I fill his bottle with water and put it into his rucksack along with some fruit and a packet of biscuits. By the time it starts to get dark and Jess will need to bring him home, the police will be here. Noah can't come back to that. He can't see what his mother has done. But I can't think of any of that now. I just need to get my son out of here.

I change Noah's shoes, taking the muddy trainers and hiding them away so that Jess won't see them when she arrives. I find his raincoat and put it on him ready, hoping the skies will stay clear. On the coat hooks, I notice the gap where Reka's raincoat and hoodies had recently hung. A wave of nausea wracks my body, and I lurch forward, putting a palm flat to the wall to steady myself.

'Daddy.'

'I'm okay,' I say quickly, raising a hand in Noah's direction as he appears behind me. 'I'm sorry. I'm okay. Everything's going to be okay.'

But it is not. Nothing is okay. Nothing will ever be okay again.

'Can you do a job for me?' I ask him, needing to keep him away from the garden and from his mother. 'Can you go and stand by the front window and call me when you see Jess's car? It's the red one, remember.'

Noah wanders off into the living room, and I go back to the kitchen. In the garden, Suzanna doesn't seem to have moved from the spot where I last saw her. As I stand here looking at her, it occurs to me that I don't know her. I had thought her one thing; she has instantly become another. Or maybe she didn't become it. Maybe this is what she's always been, but she managed to conceal it.

When was the last time I saw Reka? I think back, trying to focus. It was on Saturday evening. I spoke to her out on the driveway, before I left for the charity gala. She'd just been out for a run. She adjusted my tie after telling me it was wonky, though she'd got the word wrong. Wonksided, that was what she'd said. I'd told her it was either wonky or lopsided... she couldn't have both. We'd laughed at her mistake. Suzanna had been in the window upstairs watching us, though I don't know whether she realised either of us was aware of the fact.

I wonder now whether from her position at the window that evening, she had seen that moment play out differently. Surely she didn't think there was something going on between Reka and me? But even if she had, this isn't how Suzanna would react. She's never been a jealous person. She isn't a violent person. She hates to even get dragged into a disagreement.

'Daddy.'

I hear Noah's voice calling me from the living room, and when I go back into the hallway, I see the red of Jess's car through the frosted glass of the front door. Noah comes to the living room doorway, clutching his beagle in one hand and his rucksack in the other.

'This is going to be an adventure,' I tell him, trying to fire some excitement into my voice. 'You get to go in Jess's car.'

I open the front door, barely able to make eye contact with her. 'Thank you for this,' I mutter, as I go to my own car and take out Noah's booster seat. I put it into her car before ushering Noah over.

'Is everything okay?'

'Fine.'

She checks Noah again before mouthing, 'Is she hurt?'

She means Suzanna. I shake my head.

'If you need me, just call.' She leans forward and puts her head to one side. 'Hey, mister,' she says to Noah. 'Want to show me this new helter-skelter slide everyone's talking about?'

I get Noah into his seat and kiss his forehead. 'Have fun, mate.'

'You know I'm always here for you both, don't you?' Jess says once Noah's car door is closed.

She waits for a response, but I can't give her one. 'I'll call you,' I say, and I watch as she gets into her car and drives away with my son, feeling sick at the choices I've made and the prospect of what awaits me in the garden.

When I get back out there, Suzanna is still sitting in the churned-up soil. Reka's headband is a metre away from her. I stare at the flower bed, not wanting to linger on what I know now must be the truth. Reka is here with us, also just metres away.

'Can you tell me what happened?'

I try to stay calm. If I remain impassive and don't press her too hard, Suzanna might tell me everything. All I need is the truth. All I need is to hear her say this isn't true. Because it can't be. Surely.

'I'm not sure. It's all a bit of a blur. We had an argument. After you left for that fundraiser.'

'On Saturday? This happened on Saturday?'

I try to keep the tremor from my voice. Nothing makes sense, and yet... it all does.

But this is madness. This is Suzanna. Though I've known for a long time that my wife hides a darkness, the extent of which maybe even she's not yet aware. Perhaps none of us knows exactly what she's capable of.

'You said I needed help. She told me that was what you'd said.'

I bite my lip. I remember the comment, how easily it had escaped me. I love Suzanna. I just wanted to help her. That's all I've ever wanted. But she needs something bigger than me, something I can't offer her. It hadn't meant any more than what was said.

'What happened?'

'I pushed her. I didn't mean to hurt her. She hit her head on the door frame. I panicked.'

Suzanna recounts events slowly, removed from the words that leave her mouth. They don't really seem to make any sense.

'I don't understand. Where did this happen?'

'On the landing,' she tells me. 'At the top of the stairs.'

'You need to get up,' I tell her, because all I can think of is Reka buried in the ground beneath her. Beneath me. I try to remember how she looked on Saturday when I last saw her, but all I can picture is how she might look now, her skin grey and marbled with the drain of death, her hair matted with damp earth.

My hands have gone numb, pins and needles tearing painfully under my skin.

'You pushed her?'

'I didn't mean to. I just wanted to get past.'

Did Reka fall down the stairs, is that what Suzanna is trying to tell me? Because people don't die from bumping into a door. I try to imagine how easily it might happen, a shove to get her out of the way that led to a fall down the staircase and a fatal head injury. It must have been an accident. This isn't Suzanna. She isn't capable of this.

Yet recently, she has spoken more of the visions that plague her. Jess knows so much more than I do. Client confidentiality means she will never reveal to me the things that have been discussed during their sessions, but I see in both their eyes that there's so much more than I realise. I think Suzanna has feared that had I known everything that went on inside her head, I might have left her. Would we ever love anyone so fully if we had a window to all their thoughts?

'Here,' I say, extending a hand. 'Please, Suzanna. It's starting to rain.'

A fat drop lands on my shoulder as I say it. I think about Noah and Jess, probably not yet as far as the park. She might bring him back here too soon. I need to get Suzanna away from this garden. I need to call the police.

'Tell me what happened.'

'I just did,' she says sharply. She puts her hands over her ears and shuts her eyes tightly, her face scrunched at the sound of whatever fills her head. This is how I used to find her in those early days after Annabelle was born. She would sit in the corner of our daughter's bedroom, knees tucked to her chest, face in her hands. Annabelle would be in her cot, safe but ignored. I thought we were helping her, Jess and I, but she clearly needed so much more than we were able to offer her.

An hour after seeing her like that, maybe two, I would find Suzanna in the kitchen preparing dinner with the radio turned up, singing along carelessly as though nothing had happened.

'She was at the bottom of the stairs,' she says, the words muffled, her face lowered to her knees. 'I'd gone into Noah's bedroom after the argument. I thought if she told anyone what had happened, they would take him away from me. I couldn't lose another child. I just lay with him in the bed. I must have fallen asleep... I don't remember. When I came out to talk to her, I thought she'd be in her room. But she was at the bottom of the stairs. There was no blood. I remember thinking that was strange. And then I panicked. I couldn't lose him. Not Noah too.'

I want to say something conciliatory to her, to lie that everything is going to be okay. But I can't. It's not. And when I look at my wife, I find myself looking at a stranger. She's been acting for these past few days as though everything has been normal... or as normal as they get for us, at least. She's spoken about Reka as though she's seen her.

'Why haven't you said anything before now?'

'I've heard her,' she says quickly. 'Upstairs, listening to music in her room. Playing in the garden with Noah. I saw her earlier... I spoke to her in the kitchen.'

Beneath the rain-soaked T-shirt that clings to my skin, the blood running through my veins has turned cold. 'What do you mean? You can't have. You just said this happened on Saturday.'

Suzanna has her head in her hands, her fingers gripped tightly at her temples. Her cheeks are flushed with the cold, and tiny rivulets of rainwater run down the back of her neck, snaking beneath her sweater.

'Was it like before? When you used to hear Annabelle?'

She nods.

In those first days and weeks after Annabelle's death, Suzanna would respond to the sound of our daughter's cries. Jess reassured me that it was a normal reaction, a confusion of the brain having not yet accepted the reality of our loss. We'd seen this kind of trauma response from her before, in the weeks after she'd given birth to Annabelle. Her labour was long and the delivery complicated. She fell into a depression that seemed to have a vice-like grip over her, but there was more to it than that. Somehow, Suzanna just wasn't Suzanna. And try as she did to conceal the fact, I'm not convinced I ever saw a real glimpse of her true self again after that.

'Why didn't you talk to me?'

'I'm talking to you now.'

And just like that, she switches herself off from me again, as she does so often, disappearing into a world of which I've never been a part.

We sit in silence for a while before I tell her what I know I must. 'I'm going to have to call the police – you know that, don't you?'

Suzanna nods. There is no attempt to dissuade me. Nor does she try to make any excuses. 'I'm sorry,' is all she says.

How could I have missed the fact that something was so very wrong? Distractions, I reason with myself, trying to appease myself for my own absence, one I know has been physical and emotional. I might accuse Suzanna of existing in a bubble that shuts me out, but the truth is, I'm no different. Since Annabelle's death, I've been here but not. Present in body but absent in mind, because showing up would mean acknowledging the truth of what happened that day, and not just the facts of our daughter's death but the reality of what I've felt towards my wife since it happened. I've tried to keep myself busy because I've known that if I stopped, the ground beneath my feet would start to collapse, and that I'd collapse along with it.

I push myself up, my limbs feeling as though they've aged two decades since I arrived home. I pull my phone from my pocket and head back towards the house, where the signal is always better. I call 999. Tell them that our nanny is buried in one of the flower beds in my garden. That my wife is with me... that she's told me what happened. The call handler remains calm and impassive in the way they must all be trained, but I know she must be twistedly elated with the surrealness of it all, the fact that this call has come in on her line and during her shift and thank goodness for something headline-worthy to break the monotony of her afternoon.

When the call has ended, I go into the house and unlock the front door, leaving it ajar.

Back in the garden, Suzanna hasn't moved.

'Do you remember the moment she fell?' I ask her as I sit back beside her in the now-wet soil, the rain pelting her bare shoulder where her sweater has slipped.

'Will you make sure Noah knows I love him?'

I move my hand to hers and take her icy fingers in mine. I say nothing because there's nothing I can guarantee. An unspoken promise is better than a broken one.

Suzanna is the first to pull away, letting her hand slip from mine. Together we sit silently, our palms pressed sunken in the soil, the rain falling on us while we wait for the police to arrive.

TWENTY-TWO
WEDNESDAY

The rising scream of a siren pierces the late-afternoon silence, and a part of me expects Suzanna to get up and try to make a run for it. But she doesn't. She continues to sit quietly, silently awaiting her fate, while I sit beside her, an unnecessary warden. Tyres screech to a stop on the gravel driveway. We hear voices, doors being slammed, and within moments, Suzanna, Reka and I are no longer alone.

I'm not sure what I'm expecting when the police arrive, but it isn't this. Everything is unnaturally calm, strangers moving through the house and across the garden as though they're familiar with the place. In this moment, I realise this is no longer a home. Not our home. I've wondered so many times since Annabelle's death whether this place could ever again be what it had once promised, but this is the final answer. It's starting to feel like we were doomed from the day we moved in here.

And Reka... God, I wish we had never replied to her job application, that we had never brought her into our chaos.

'Mr Cross?'

A plain-clothes police officer crosses the wet lawn. I stand

and wipe my hands on my trousers, which are soaked through to my skin.

The officer looks at my wife and for a moment no one knows what to say. They'll have already been given the details I offered the call handler.

'I'm DI Harris,' he says.

I glance at Suzanna, who doesn't seem to have acknowledged his presence. We move a few metres away, though Suzanna must surely still be able to hear us. As we speak, a couple of uniformed officers move towards the flower bed.

'You made the 999 call?' the detective asks me.

I nod. Behind him, I see one of the uniformed officers holding Suzanna by the arm, helping her up from the ground. Without context, my wife looks like a victim. With her soil-stained clothing and her wet hair stuck to her face in messy tendrils, anyone might think that a crime has befallen her. The officer might be seen as assisting her rather than preparing for her arrest.

'I'm going to need some information from you. The woman in the flower bed... you told the call handler she's your nanny, is that correct?'

I nod. 'Reka. Reka Bako.'

'How long has she been working for you?'

'Just over four months. And she's been living here since she took up the job.'

The detective watches his colleague speak to Suzanna. I wonder what's being said. Suzanna seems barely responsive.

'Is Ms Bako British?'

'She's Hungarian.'

'Does she have any relatives in the UK?'

I shake my head.

'We'll need you to give a full statement at the station, Mr Cross, but for now I need some of the facts. You said your wife just told you this afternoon that she killed Ms Bako?'

With his words comes a rush of blood to my head. Spoken aloud, it doesn't sound real. It can't be true. But I nod because that's all I can bring myself to do. For a moment, I leave the garden. The sights and sounds around me dissolve, and I am timeless, nowhere, without either thought or feeling.

'Is there anything we should know about your wife, Mr Cross? Is she on any medication? Any history of violence? Mr Cross?'

'Sorry. Yes. I mean, yes, she takes medication for her anxiety. Depression. Last year...' But I can't finish what I was going to say. Everything will come out once Suzanna is taken in for interview. They'll pick apart our lives with the most brutal of details. 'She isn't violent. We've been together for almost seven years. I've never known her to be violent. She's the opposite – she's kind and compassionate and patient. She would never do anything to hurt anyone.'

Yet here we are. This detective and me, standing in the rain, looking at my kind and compassionate and patient wife being helped from the ground where she buried our child's nanny.

Before either of us has time to move, I throw up on the lawn. My body doubles forward with the force of it, and a searing pain like a burst of flame rushes from my chest to my head as I stand bent at the waist, my face hovering over the puddle of vomit that lies at my feet.

'I'm sorry,' I mutter.

I register the look of barely restrained disgust on the detective's face. 'Do you need some water?' he asks impassively.

'No,' I tell him, turning away, wiping my mouth with my sleeve. 'I'm sorry. I...'

But I don't know what the right thing to say is. Everything I say will be recorded, possibly later used against Suzanna. Even against me.

'Is it just the two of you living here?' the detective asks.

'No. We have a son, Noah. Someone's looking after him.'

'Can you tell me, Mr Cross, what your wife told you this afternoon, before you made the 999 call?'

'That she and Reka had argued on Saturday evening. That she'd pushed past her, but she hadn't meant to bump into her so hard. She said that Reka had fallen down the stairs.'

'On Saturday? But she only mentioned this to you now?'

'I thought Reka had been avoiding us. Me, in particular.'

The detective's left eyebrow raises. 'Why would that have been?'

'There was an accident on Monday. My son fell off the climbing frame over there. Suzanna called me on her way to the hospital, and when I got there, I asked where Reka had been when it happened. I thought she'd been looking after him. Suzanna made it sound as though she'd just abandoned Noah after he'd fallen.'

'But Ms Bako hadn't been there at all. She couldn't have been.'

It sounds like a statement rather than a question, so I say nothing. But the past few days begin to come back to me, every conversation I've had with Suzanna returning with a different sound. She knew. All the times she'd spoken of Reka as though she was simply somewhere else, seemingly trying to evade the consequences of her negligence, Suzanna had known that she was gone. She knew what she'd done.

'It's not unusual for me not to see Reka much during the week,' I find myself explaining. 'I work early... I'm usually out of the house by five thirty. Reka has Noah until four-ish and she tends to keep herself to herself in the evenings, to give us family time.'

I stop talking. At some point, I'm going to have to admit that I had told Suzanna to sack Reka, or that I would do it. I don't think the fact that we'd wanted her gone is going to help either of us. I see a white-clad figure move through the kitchen. Forensics. I glance down the garden at the flower bed. 'I just thought she was avoiding us. And then last night, when I saw her things were gone, I thought she'd realised she couldn't stay any longer, after Noah's accident.'

'Her things were gone?'

The detective reads the panic on my face. The laptop... the phone charger... her trainers and coat... where the hell are they? If Susanna had moved those things, why leave all Reka's other personal belongings behind? If she'd wanted to hide what she'd done, why did she start digging up the flower bed this afternoon?

I feel a second wave of nausea rush through me.

'Perhaps this had better all wait for the station,' DI Harris says, and I can't miss his abrasive tone of voice. The more I talk, the more guilty he believes me. But I can't incriminate myself in this. Noah is about to lose his mother... I can't let him lose me too.

I don't get a chance to react to this: the second officer approaches us, her hand still on Suzanna's arm, directing her. 'Boss,' she says, 'you'd better check it out.' She gestures to the flower bed, and DI Harris leaves my side.

My wife hasn't looked up from the ground. She can't look at me. She can't bring herself to look at anyone. But I watch as the DI moves among the forensic investigators, crouching when instructed, not staying there longer than he needs to. He straightens himself and turns. Gives a nod.

'I'm going to read you your rights now, okay?' the woman says, speaking to Suzanna as though she's a child or hard of hearing. 'Suzanna Cross, you are under arrest for the murder of Reka Bako. You do not need to say anything...'

I don't hear the rest. The sounds around me start to blur and fade, like I'm being pulled under water and the world above the surface has become inaudible. I think of Suzanna and me standing at the washing machine just days ago, of how I'd naïvely commented on how Reka needed to clean up after herself. She wasn't being slovenly; she was already gone. And Suzanna had known that all long.

I look at my wife being led towards the house in handcuffs and I realise I don't know her any more. Perhaps I've never known her. And I can't shake off the overriding thought that rises above every other: that if I hadn't gone out on Saturday night, none of this would have happened. Reka would still be alive.

TWENTY-THREE

WEDNESDAY

The tea in the cardboard cup in front of me tastes like dishwater. I'm sitting in an interview room, alone with my thoughts, the only other sound the incessant buzzing that has rung in my head since I followed Noah into the garden earlier this afternoon. I think of him now with Jess. She seems to have assumed that Suzanna's been taken ill, and that I don't want Noah made aware of anything. She told me she'd take him to a supermarket and buy him a pair of pyjamas, and that he could stay overnight in her spare bedroom.

My son should be at home, where I know he's safe, but the irony of the notion momentarily blows all other thoughts aside. Are any of us safe anywhere?

I get a feeling like I'm being watched, though there are no windows in the room. Then I spot it: the camera in the corner of the ceiling, pointed down at the table where I'm sitting. It's common practice, I know; I assume every police interview room across the country has a camera installed. But it still feels disconcerting to know I'm being observed as I sit here waiting, not knowing what's going on on the other side of these four walls.

Suzanna is somewhere in the station, too – possibly just a few corridors away from me. I wonder whether she's spoken to anyone yet, and what's been said. But I don't need to wait long for answers. As my thoughts turn to Noah and how unsettled he might be with neither Suzanna nor me there for his bedtime, DI Harris enters the room, accompanied by the female officer who earlier read my wife her rights. He introduces her as DC Western.

'Is Suzanna okay?' I look from one officer to the other, but neither of them replies – no one speaks until the tape recorder is running.

'Interview with Matthew Cross commencing at seven forty p.m.,' says DI Harris. 'The date is Wednesday, twelfth March.'

'Am I under arrest? Do I need a solicitor?'

'Do you feel you need a solicitor?'

The question is loaded. If I answer yes, it implies that I'm guilty of something. I shake my head.

'For the purposes of the recording, Mr Cross has declined a solicitor. You're not under arrest. Your wife has made a full confession. She says you knew nothing about what happened until this afternoon.'

I lower my head. With my hands clasped in my lap, I try to hold it together. I have to for Noah's sake. When I look up, DC Western is looking at me with sympathy, though DI Harris appears to remain unconvinced.

'Can I see her?' I ask.

'I'm afraid that won't be possible,' DC Western says. 'Not at the moment. We're going to need you to make a full statement – do you feel up to that now?'

I nod. She talks me through what needs to be included, and for the next half an hour I talk, giving them details of Reka and how she came into our lives, her relationship with Noah and with Suzanna. Her relationship with me. I answer their questions as best I can, ever fearful that anything I say may inadvertently make things somehow even worse for Suzanna. Because there's still a part of me that feels this is all a bad dream, that I'll wake and things will be different – our lives still broken by the loss of Annabelle, but the three of us still a unit, still clinging on to what remains of us.

'Suzanna's been having therapy since Annabelle died. She'd suffered with depression before but never really sought help for it. Her therapist knows more than I do – she'll be able to give you the details. Will it help her?'

'Help Suzanna?' DI Harris's left eyebrow arches. The look says enough.

'I'm not suggesting it excuses anything. But this isn't Suzanna... She's not a bad person.'

Silence hangs in the air between us. Things are as bad as they can get.

'Our daughter's death destroyed her. She's never forgiven herself for what happened.'

In a moment, I imagine they will ask me to go into the details of the day Annabelle left our lives. Perhaps they somehow already know, yet I will be required to relive it all again, a slow and drawn-out torture that always feels as though it will suffocate me. A quick internet search of either my name or Suzanna's will lead them quickly to what they're looking for, though I know they'll want to hear it from me, and then, I presume, they'll want to hear it from Suzanna.

When the winter fitness challenge I'd started in November went viral, our story quickly followed. As a result, our life was dissected on social media by people who knew nothing about us. I read far more than Suzanna ever did. Her name was torn to pieces, blamed by many for what had happened to our daughter. She was accused of being negligent. An unfit mother. Her name was used in the same sentence as the word 'murderer'. The invisible masses debated whether we should have been allowed to keep Noah in our care.

I'd needed somewhere to channel my grief, an outlet that would keep my mind so occupied it wouldn't have time to linger on thoughts of what had happened. I'd needed a distraction from the first Christmas that was lurking just around the corner, with no idea how any of us were supposed to survive it. And yet, my desire for some kind of a purpose brought us more negative attention than I could ever have anticipated, and in trying to meet my own needs, I failed Suzanna.

'Are you able to tell us about your daughter's death?' DC Western asks. 'I know this must be difficult for you.'

For the next twenty minutes, I talk them through that day, from leaving for work early in the morning to getting home in the afternoon to an unusually quiet house. I give them the details of the things I noticed when I first walked through the door: Noah's balance bike in the hallway alongside his sister's pram, the half-eaten baby biscuit that had been abandoned on the pink blanket embroidered with her name. I'd taken my shoes off and gone down to the kitchen, expecting to find them outside in the garden. But the back doors were locked and there was no one there. The dishwasher was open, loaded with dirty dishes: among them, Noah's blue breakfast bowl with the cartoon elephant balancing a ball. There were no other dishes or utensils on the worktops, and it didn't look as though anyone had eaten since breakfast.

When I went back into the hallway, I realised the doors to both living rooms were closed. This was unusual because Noah always had trouble with the handles by himself; they were the original doorknobs, stiff to twist open, so Suzanna and I never fully closed them. When I opened the door to the main living room, the first thing I saw was Annabelle's rocker chair by the sofa. She wasn't in it, but the little plastic star-shaped music box that was fixed to the handlebar across the front was still playing soft piano music, almost eerie in her absence.

'And then I saw her,' I hear myself telling the detectives.

'Suzanna was sitting at the far end of the sofa, holding her close to her chest. Too close. I couldn't see Annabelle's face, only Suzanna's. She was sort of blank, like she wasn't there. I don't think she'd even seen me, despite my being right in front of her. And then I realised that Annabelle wasn't moving at all. Even while she was asleep, there'd be movement of some kind, even just the rise and fall of her chest. And she would never sleep like that on either of us, with her face hidden like that.'

'Mr Cross... you can stop if you need a moment.'

I can't see DC Western. Through the blur of tears that blinds me, she has become a distorted shape at the other side of the table. I wipe the back of my hand across each eye in turn, and the detectives come back into focus.

'I didn't know at first what had happened. Then Suzanna told me that she'd woken up and found Noah holding his sister... that she wasn't moving. She said he wouldn't speak to her, wouldn't tell her what had happened, that when she asked him what had happened, he just started crying. I asked where Noah was, and Suzanna told me she didn't know. I ran through the house looking for him and eventually found him in Annabelle's bedroom, curled up in a ball at the end of her cot. He looked so tiny lying there... like a baby again. I asked him what had happened, but he wouldn't tell me. It was like he couldn't speak – he was terrified. I should have been there that day. If I'd taken better care of her, none of this would have happened. Annabelle... Reka...'

I stop talking, aware I've said too much. In their eyes, I can see what they're thinking, the exchange that's taking place between their silent glances. Two deaths. A house cursed with tragedy. A family plagued by loss.

Surely lightning doesn't strike in the same place twice.

TWENTY-FOUR

THURSDAY

I called a solicitor after my interview was over, and at just after midnight, I get to Jess's house. The soft glow of lamplight soaks through the curtains of the downstairs front window, but other than this the house is bathed in darkness. I don't need to call her number to ask her to let me in; I see her face at the window and realise she's waited up for me, watching out for my car on the street. The last place I want to be tonight is here.

'I should have called,' I say quietly as I click the front door softly shut behind me. 'I'm sorry... I didn't think.' I can barely bring myself to look at her or at the house. I just want to be in my own home, or anywhere but here, and not about to have the conversation I know will follow.

'It's fine. And Noah's fine. I've been up to check on him a couple of times, but he's fast asleep.'

I take off my shoes by the front door and put them on the shoe rack next to hers and Noah's. It all feels oddly domestic and inappropriate.

'How's Suzanna?'

'I don't know. I wasn't allowed to see her.'

'Are you okay?'

'No.' My eyes flit up to the landing, to the door of the spare bedroom where Noah lies sleeping, oblivious to his little life's latest tragedy. 'But I'm going to have to be, aren't I?'

I follow her into the living room, and she closes the door so that should Noah wake up, he won't hear any of our conversation. I can't even begin to think how I'm going to tell him that his mother is gone from our lives for a while, and that I'm not sure for how long. Will she get bail while she awaits trial? I doubt it. And would it be the right thing for our son if she did? It'll be too confusing and upsetting for him, to have her back for a while just to lose her again.

And is he even safe around her after what she's done?

The thought hits me with the force of a brick.

'God, Matt, you need to sit down.' Jess's hand grabs for my arm. I pull away from her and sit on the sofa, almost collapsing into it.

'She said she was there, Jess. She made out like she and Reka had seen each other... like everything was normal. How could she lie to me like that? How could she behave like nothing had happened knowing what she'd done?'

'Have you eaten anything?'

The last thing I can think about is food. 'I'm fine.'

'You need something. Even if it's just a piece of toast, please let me make you something.'

She goes to the kitchen, leaving me alone with my thoughts – and I find myself wishing I could escape my own brain. No matter the different ways I turn it over in my mind, I can't make any sense of what Suzanna has done. I've known for a long time that she's plagued by doubts and self-loathing, that her mind sometimes takes her to places she never even wants to confide in me about. But this is a leap my own brain could never have made, that the woman I met all those years ago might be capable of such deception and such apparent disregard for another person's life.

I get up and go down the hallway to the kitchen, unable to be alone with myself a moment longer.

'Jess, we need to—'

'Try to eat this,' she says, thrusting a plate of buttered toast towards me as she cuts my sentence dead. 'The kettle's on. I'll add sugar. You need it.'

I put the plate on the worktop beside me as she sets about making tea. I find myself wondering whether Suzanna has been given something to eat or drink. I've known her to forget to eat in the past, a symptom of the depression that at its worst makes her neglect her own basic needs.

'We need to talk about what happened,' I say.

'What happened?'

She turns away from me to return the lid to the butter.

'Jess, please—'

'Do you think she really doesn't remember what happened?'

I watch her take the butter back to the fridge. 'I don't know. When she spoke about it, she sounded as though she wasn't sure of anything.'

Jess closes the fridge door. 'Exactly. And I know it's the same for you too, isn't it? You don't talk about it because I know you're trying to stay strong for Suzanna, but I've seen it, Matthew. Sometimes, it's like you drift off somewhere else, into your own world. Are you even sure of what's real or not when you're in those moments?'

I can't answer her because the truth is I'm not sure. She's right that it happens, but I don't want her to regard me with the same vulnerability she sees in Suzanna. Whatever I've experienced, I know it's not the same as what she's been going through.

'It's a trauma response. What the two of you have gone through... it's the worst thing imaginable. And I think your responses to it may be more similar than either of you realises.'

I don't know what to think. But she's right about one thing, at least... sometimes, I'm so detached that I lose whole moments of time.

'You got the window fixed,' I say, desperate to change the subject.

She nods. 'Tell me what happened this afternoon.' She brings a cup of tea over to me and sits opposite.

And then I tell her. From arriving back at the house after the run to giving my statement at the station. All the while, Jess listens intently, like I'm one of her clients offloading my life's burdens.

'I can't stop thinking about Reka's laptop being gone from the house,' I admit, slumping on to a stool at the breakfast bar. 'Suzanna must have disposed of it. But why do that? It's all so calculated. I tried to defend her at the station – I made sure they knew about her depression and the bereavement – but the whole time I was trying to make excuses for her, I realised that's all they were. She buried that poor girl in the garden, for Christ's sake.'

Jess watches me silently and says nothing.

'Accidents happen,' I continue, my thoughts spilling from me. 'She might have shoved past her like she said, she might have knocked into Reka harder than she'd meant to. Perhaps the fall really was an accident. But to then try to conceal her body... to get rid of specific items to make it seem like she'd left us in a hurry. She stood in Reka's bedroom with me, talking about her leaving. She put her in the ground where our son plays, for fuck's sake.' I gasp for air like a drowning man. 'I'm sorry,' I say, realising how loud my voice has risen. 'I just... None of it makes sense. This isn't Suzanna.'

'She's been under a lot of pressure.'

'Seriously? Pressure doesn't make people violent. It doesn't make people devious and calculated. It doesn't make someone bury their nanny in the fucking garden.'

I shut my eyes and grit my teeth, trying to manage the anger that threatens to burst from me. Because it's not just Suzanna I'm furious with. It's not just Suzanna I can no longer trust. I can't even trust myself any more.

'But it can make people do stupid, inadvisable things,' Jess says. 'Reckless, dangerous things. Pressure makes people make bad decisions in split-second moments.'

She holds my gaze for too long before I break away from it.

'It took more than a split second to get a shovel, dig up the flower bed and drag Reka's body from the house.'

As I speak the words, I feel a surge of sickness swell in my stomach, just as it did this afternoon when I'd been with DI Harris. The smell of the butter that's soaked into the toast makes my gut churn.

There have been so many times over the past year that I've thought I wanted my marriage to Suzanna to be over. On so many nights I've lain awake wondering how we're supposed to go on in the shadow of what happened to our baby, with Suzanna's guilt and my own colliding and repelling. I doubted we could ever be the parents Noah needed – not together, at least. But I never imagined the end in this way. Not like this. With Suzanna in custody, I realise just how much we need her. The real her... not the version of her that's committed this unthinkable crime.

But I suppose that's just it. Maybe this is the real Suzanna.

'I don't want to think of her in this way, but how else am I supposed to think?'

'Suzanna has blackouts.'

I feel my eyes narrow. 'What?'

Jess exhales slowly, puffing out her cheeks. 'I've never told you because it's not my place to. I'm bound by patient confidentiality. I encouraged her to tell you about them, but it was her choice to make, and she wasn't ready. I assumed she would at some point.'

'Blackouts? But I've never known her to faint. And she

doesn't drink... I thought blackouts were associated with intoxication? The drugs she's been taking—'

'Are perhaps enough to have caused some of the blackouts, if it is the case that she's been accidentally overdosing. But they've been happening for longer than she's been taking some of the meds. We're not talking about fainting here. We're talking about mental blackouts... memory lapses. I believe it's more to do with the extremity of her anxiety, coupled with exhaustion.'

I feel a coldness creep into my bones. 'So what are you saying... that she does things she can't remember doing?'

She meets my eye for a little too long, and I see the silent message that she passes. *Just like you, Matthew*, it seems to say. *Just like you, if only you knew it.*

'Sometimes. Or she can't recall the details of conversations, or she'll believe they never happened at all. It can happen, with extreme trauma such as yours.'

There is silence for a moment as her words are absorbed into the air between us. *Trauma such as yours.*

'So you're able to help her?' I say, as her focus on me becomes uncomfortable. 'If the police know about this, they'll realise she may not even have any memory of it happening. If she was experiencing a blackout at the time, she can't be responsible for what happened, can she?'

But as the words leave me, I hear the hopeless desperation of them. Jess is looking at me pityingly. But there's something else there too. Disbelief. She's right. Why would I be looking for ways to save Suzanna after this?

'She's experienced this kind of blackout within our sessions,' she says softly. 'There have been things she's admitted to me that she has no recollection of saying... things she's later vehemently denied.'

'Things? What things?'

Jess gets up from the table and goes to put the milk carton

back in the fridge. But I know it's just an excuse to look away, to avoid eye contact with me.

'Jess. Please. There's no time for secrets any more.'

I realise the irony of my words as they're spoken, but Jess looks away, both of us choosing to ignore what stands invisibly in front of us. I get up from the stool and go over to her.

'Jess.' I reach for her shoulder and pull her around to me, too hard. *As simple as a push*, I think. How easy not to realise one's own strength.

But my hand is still on her shoulder, and I can't let go. 'Admitted to what, Jess? What did Suzanna tell you? If you won't tell me, you're going to have to tell the police. They're going to want to know the details of everything that she shared in those sessions – confidentiality doesn't exist here any more.'

Jess glances at the hand that grips her shoulder.

'Don't do this, Matthew.'

'But if it relates to Reka... if it's relevant to anything else...'

I can't bring myself to say it, but her unspoken name sits between us, tainting the air with an accusation. Jess takes my hand and prises my fingers from her shoulder, shoving my arm away with a stare that promises me that if I ever touch her again, it won't just be Suzanna heading for prison.

'I'm trying to help you, Matthew. Please don't make it difficult for me.'

She leaves, and I wait in the kitchen for a moment, hearing her footsteps on the stairs and then the landing. When I go up to the spare bedroom, Noah is sleeping soundly, just as Jess had said. He looks tiny in the double bed, curled into a ball close to the wall with the duvet almost concealing him completely. I have nothing with me to change into, so I get into bed still in the running gear I was wearing yesterday afternoon. I put a hand on my son's shoulder, feeling the warmth of him. Tomorrow, or maybe the next day, I'm going to have to find a way to tell him that his mother won't be with us for a while. I'm going to have to find a way to explain Reka's absence too. These things are too much for a four-year-old child to have to comprehend.

I curl against my son's sleeping body, feeling the heat radiate from him as his shoulder gently rises and falls with the rhythm of his breathing. When I close my eyes, unable to find any rest, I see Suzanna sitting on a bench in a prison cell... Jess lying a couple of rooms away in her bed... Annabelle as I had seen her that day, clutched so close to her mother's chest that, at first, I thought she'd suffocated her.

Suzanna has lied about so many things. So just what the hell did she admit to Jess during those sessions?

TWENTY-FIVE
THURSDAY

Jess holds her sessions with clients in the back room of her beautiful Victorian terraced property, from where we could be a million miles from the rest of the house. The walls are painted a deep green and there are numerous houseplants in large pots. There's a bookcase stocked with therapy guides and self-help manuals, with the only other furniture her chair and the sofa. It is easy to feel comfortable here – a cool room in the summer, a warm room in the depth of winter. I wonder how many confessions she has listened to in this room. She must have witnessed so much more than she's ever revealed: the imminent end of marriages, the prelude to self-harm, fears and desires, grievances and regrets.

From the living room, the theme tune of one of Noah's favourite cartoons rings down the hallway. Jess is in the kitchen, making him some breakfast. I push the door closed and take my ringing mobile from my pocket. Last night, after I was interviewed by police, I contacted Jonathan Hart, the solicitor that Suzanna and I had met following Annabelle's death. He knows our family history well enough that I trust him more than anyone to deal with what we're facing now, though he made it clear in no uncertain terms when we spoke last night that the outlook doesn't look good for Suzanna.

I'm not sure I slept for more than a few minutes at a time last night. Every time my body tried to pull my brain into the abyss, I was jolted back to consciousness by the image of Reka's headband lying in the churned-up soil of the flower bed, my wife sitting feet away on the damp earth. The more I think of this past week, the worse it all becomes, as if it could get any more nightmarish.

I answer quickly, grateful for the distraction.

'She's been charged,' the solicitor tells me.

'Already? But she hasn't even been there twenty-four hours yet.'

'They don't need any more time. With a confession, a charge can be made straight away.'

'What about bail? Is it a possibility?'

'Possibly. But look... until a psychiatric assessment is completed—'

'A psychiatric assessment? No one mentioned this last night.'

'It's there to help her. When this goes for sentencing, her medical history is going to come under scrutiny. The more that's understood about her mental health, the better.'

'What... you mean like mitigating circumstances?'

'Let's not jump ahead to that just yet. Try to take this day by day.'

'So, what can I do today? Because it feels as though I'm just sitting around waiting for something to happen. I can't even take my son back to his own home. My house is a fucking crime scene.'

The door creaks open. Jess is holding a cup of tea, her face creased with concern at the sound of my raised voice.

'I'm sorry,' I say to Jonathan. 'I just need to be doing something. Anything useful.'

'Focus on your son. Let me deal with Suzanna for now. The police are going to get access to her GP records... You said she has a therapist as well?'

I glance at Jess. 'Yes, that's right.'

'They'll want to speak to her. Look... Suzanna's confessed to murder. I can argue a case for manslaughter, but that's the best we can hope for at this stage. I'm sorry, Matthew, but we need to be realistic.'

I end the call, and Jess closes the door. She hands me a cup of tea.

'Solicitor?' she asks.

I nod. 'For what he's worth now.' I lower myself on to the sofa, gripping the mug between both hands. 'They're going to do a psychiatric assessment on Suzanna. They'll want to speak to you, about her mental health.'

'All sounds like standard practice. You and Noah can stay here for as long as you need to.'

I mumble a thank you, because that's what I'm supposed to do. But I don't want to stay here. I don't want Noah staying here. We should both be at home... if we still had a home to go to.

'I can't. And anyway, it's a lot to ask.'

'You didn't ask.'

'I don't know how long the house will be kept a crime scene.' The words taste like bile in my mouth. It's our family home, the place where all our collective dreams were supposed to be made a reality.

'The other night—'

'It's forgotten,' she says, dismissing my attempt to raise the subject for a second time. 'You've been under a lot of strain. Don't worry about that now... you've got enough to think about. Does the solicitor think Suzanna has a chance of getting out on bail?'

'Not yet.' I press my fingertips to my forehead, trying to

push back the throbbing ache that rests there. 'Why am I trying to get her help? She killed a woman. Accident or not, she caused the death of someone who trusted us... someone who'd come into our home to help our family. Then she tried to cover it up. She lied to my face. Perhaps she doesn't deserve to get out of there. Maybe prison is where she should be.'

Jess sits beside me and puts a hand on my arm. 'You're in shock, Matthew. This has all been dropped on you. Whatever Suzanna has done, you know it isn't her, not really.'

I feel myself stiffen at her words. It can't be justified.

'I'm thinking my own wife should be locked up, for Christ's sake. The mother of my kids.'

There's a moment of silence between us as we both absorb my casual use of the plural. Annabelle should still be here with us. The four of us, together. If Annabelle hadn't died, Reka would still be alive now too. Suzanna would be a different person... the woman she'd been before.

'There's no right or wrong way to behave or react here. You haven't had time to process any of this.'

'Do you think a case of diminished responsibility can be argued? She told me that she never meant to hurt Reka. If anything, it sounded like she'd barely shoved past her. It was a tragic accident.'

Jess is looking at me pityingly again. I know what the look says. I'm holding on to wishful thinking, letting hope obscure the facts. I see her questioning my state of mind, wondering whether I'm as unreliable a source of information as my wife is.

'You know that Suzanna's recall is affected in times of stress. If anything, if Suzanna was to withdraw her confession and this went to trial, the prosecution would likely argue that given Suzanna's inability to remember the details of events correctly, it's arguable that she shoved Reka with the intention of hurting her, but her memory has repressed the fact. This isn't me saying this, by the way,' she adds. 'I'm just trying to show you how this could pan out in court.'

In court. The words ring in my ears. It hurts to think of Suzanna being dragged through a trial, put in front of a jury; there will likely be another case of trial by media, and given our history, I doubt the keyboard warriors of social media will go kindly on her. Annabelle's death and the circumstances around it will be hauled back across our computer screens. I already know she won't cope with any of it. She'll probably end up on suicide watch.

Jess puts a hand over mine, and her touch sends a reaction snaking through my arm.

'Jess, please,' I say, pulling away from her. 'What you said in the night... about Suzanna admitting to things during sessions.'

'It's nothing like what you're thinking.' She glances to the door. 'One of us should check on Noah.'

'I'll do it.'

As I stand, she reaches again for my arm. 'Stay,' she says. 'Let me look after you both. For Noah's sake.'

I open my mouth to speak, but I'm interrupted by a call on Jess's landline ringing from the hallway. She gets up and goes to answer it, leaving me alone. I should go and check on Noah, but I'm not ready to face him again just yet. I'm going to have to lie to him, because the truth is something no child should be expected to endure.

But it's not just the thought of Suzanna's crime that holds me back from our son. I'm going to have to face him knowing I carry my own secret, knowing that every time I now look at him, I'm no better than the lie I've told. I don't know how long I can stay in Jess's house, acting like nothing happened. Like everything is normal between us... or as normal as anything can get, right now.

TWENTY-SIX

THURSDAY

At the police station, DC Western ushers me into an empty interview room and offers me tea, which I politely decline. Last night, I said too much. Today, I know I need to be mindful of every word that leaves my mouth.

'Suzanna has had an initial psychiatric assessment carried out by a doctor this morning,' she tells me.

'Is this something that normally happens?'

'Where there's a history of mental health issues, yes. And with Suzanna as she was overnight, we deemed it necessary.'

'What do you mean "as she was"? What's happened?'

'Nothing, Mr Cross. I can assure you that Suzanna is safe. But there are questions surrounding her mental health. Has your wife ever experienced any form of psychosis in the past?'

The word hits me like a punch. 'Psychosis? No. I mean, she had postnatal depression after Annabelle was born, but that's fairly common, isn't it?'

The officer looks at me disapprovingly, judgement stamped across her face. *How could you not have known?* her expression says. It was my business to know. She's right, but I was too busy trying to run away – if not physically, then in my own head, at least.

'Why are you asking about this?' I press. 'Did the doctor this morning mention psychosis?'

'Your wife's recounting of the events leading up to Reka Bako's death don't always match up. Things she told us at the house yesterday don't correlate with what she's said since. Our understanding at the moment is that she's suffered a trauma that might have impacted upon her memory. She's also mentioned hearing voices—'

'Voices?'

I feel sick. Suzanna really was hearing Reka in the house. To her, it was real. When Noah fell off the climbing frame, Suzanna must have truly believed that Reka had been in the garden with him.

'We're waiting for the results of some samples that will show whether—'

'Samples? What samples?'

'Your wife agreed to be substance tested.'

'I should have been consulted about this!' I protest. 'You're suggesting my wife has been under the influence of something, but also that she might not be in a fit state to have given an accurate or fair statement. If that's the case, how the hell can a decision have been made for her to undergo testing without my knowledge? She isn't in any position to make these decisions for herself.'

'Suzanna was of sound mind to make a decision about a blood test. Her solicitor was present.'

'But she can't have been of sound mind if you're talking about psychosis.'

My voice has risen, and the DC is giving me that disapproving look again, this time with a greater sense of warning.

'I'm sorry,' I mumble. 'I just don't see how it's relevant to what happened to Reka.'

'We need a full and accurate picture of her health, both physical and mental. I understand Suzanna's therapist is with you. She was contacted earlier this morning regarding a statement.'

'She's in the car,' I tell her. 'She'll come in when I go out – someone needs to be there with my son.'

The officer nods, and her face softens slightly, her earlier judgement slipping from her to make space for what might even be sympathy. 'Suzanna said she's a friend of the family. Is that common practice... for a therapist to be someone you're so familiar with?'

I feel a sting in my chest. She's right to query it... it isn't normal. And now I wish a different choice had been made.

'No, but it was what Suzanna wanted. Jess is a friend from university. They've known each other for twenty years. She didn't want to confide in a stranger. Look... these discrepancies in Suzanna's accounts of what happened on Saturday evening... what are they?'

'Times... places... the sequence of events.'

I sense the detective is being purposely vague, and although there was an element of sympathy from her just a moment ago, I know she's still cynical about my innocence. Beneath her fixed gaze, I find myself starting to overheat.

'And that's enough for the doctor to suspect some kind of psychosis?'

'Not that alone,' the detective says, her lips thin as she absorbs the defensiveness that we both heard in my tone.

The truth is, I'm scared. I can't be implicated in any of this, because what will happen to Noah then?

When the interview is over and I leave the station, I go back to Jess and Noah, where they're waiting for me in the car park. Noah is sitting in the front seat beside Jess, playing a game on her phone.

'I hope you don't mind,' she says, gesturing to the phone. 'I should have brought something else for him to do.'

'That was my job,' I say. I get into the back seat and lean against the headrest, the throbbing at my temples pounding in an incessant rhythm.

'Is everything okay?' Jess's eyes meet mine in the rear-view mirror.

'They want to speak to you,' I tell her, managing to evade an answer to her question.

'I know. They called. Noah, you can keep the phone for now. Do you want to head back? I can get a taxi home.'

'No. It's fine... we'll wait.'

I watch Jess walk towards the station with a knot of anxiety in my stomach. *This could be it*, I think. *The end of everything.*

I glance at Noah, absorbed by the phone screen yet not seeming to be playing the game.

'Everything's going to be all right, mate,' I tell him. Perhaps the biggest lie I've told this week... even bigger than the one I told Suzanna.

TWENTY-SEVEN
THURSDAY

I am woken by a scream. Next to me, heat radiates from Noah's small body, and his cry pierces the darkness of the room.

'Noah.' I put a hand on his shoulder, shaking him gently to wake him. 'Noah, it's okay.'

He wakes still screaming, sweat soaked through his cotton pyjama top, his face clammy and red. It reminds me so much of Suzanna and how she's so often ripped from her dreams that for a moment, I don't know how to react. I want to hold him, but something pulls me back like an invisible force.

This is my child, I tell myself. *This is Noah.*

I take him in my arms, swallowing down the uncertainty that has settled over me. I try not to see Annabelle when I look at him, but it is so, so hard not to.

His little body trembles against me as he tries to catch his breath.

'She was there.'

Noah barely speaks and so now, on the rare occasions that he does, I find myself not recognising the sound of his voice, like there's a stranger in the room with us. He must have questions, so many of them, but Noah will continue to refuse to articulate them. I don't believe for a moment that he's incapable of doing so. By the age of three, Noah had a vocabulary that was more that of a five-year-old. He was a chatty child, curious and inquisitive, always asking questions about this, that and everything, eager to learn and keen to explore. All that changed in a single afternoon. Within mere moments. It's not that Noah can't speak. He doesn't speak because he doesn't want to, having learned at such a fragile age that silence offers a semblance of control while everything else is crumbling.

'It was just a dream, lovely boy. There's nothing to be scared of.'

Despite the redness of his face, when I touch his cheek, it's cold.

'She was there,' he says again, this time with his face scrunched up, his baby teeth gritted against the words.

I wriggle down beneath the duvet so that I'm lying next to him, and I pull him closer to me. 'It's okay,' I say, and I repeat it over and over in the darkness, trying to reassure myself as much as I'm trying to reassure him. 'It was just a bad dream. You're safe now.'

But I can't shake his words from my brain. *She was there.* What is he referring to? And just how much might he have seen on Saturday night?

Suzanna said that everything had happened while Noah had been asleep, yet she would have had no way of knowing this. She would only have known him to be in bed, but for all she knew, he might have been awake. Had he heard the argument between his mother and Reka? Had he got up from bed and gone to the bedroom door? Had he eased it open and seen the push that had caused Reka to fall? He could have got back into his bed afterwards and Suzanna would have been none the wiser. She would never have known that our son had seen what she'd done.

My eyes have adjusted to the darkness, and as Noah's

tensed body begins to relax against mine, I feel us pulled into the soothing blue calmness of this room that doesn't belong to us, like being sucked into a darkened night sky and held inert within its vastness.

'Where is she?' he asks.

My heart sinks. I knew it was coming, but I'd hoped that maybe I'd get a little longer to delay the inevitable. Now, I realise I'm unprepared for the lie I'm about to have to tell.

'Mummy, you mean?'

Noah twists beside me, turning on to his side to face me. In the darkness, his little face looks even paler than usual. He looks at me with those sad grey eyes, and sadness twists in my gut like a disease.

'Reka.'

Her name in the darkness sends a shiver snaking beneath my skin, the hairs on my arms rising with the chill. Outside, on the landing, I hear the bathroom door clicking shut. Noah's scream must have woken Jess.

'She had to go away.'

'Where?'

This is the most I've heard my son speak in nearly a year, and I wonder what has made him find his voice now, after all this time. Trauma made him silent. Perhaps a second trauma is now breaking that silence.

'She had to go home,' I say, unable to look him directly in the eyes. 'You know she was from a different country, don't you? That's why she had that beautiful accent that was so different to ours.'

Had. The past tense seems to ring out in the silence, though I doubt a four-year-old would hear its implications in the way I do.

'But I'm here to look after you now, mate, okay? I'm not going to be going to work for a while. I'm going to be here for you, okay?'

He says nothing, but he moves closer to my chest, and I'm relieved that he still trusts me. I probably don't deserve it. The bathroom door is opened, and a shard of light moves across the bottom of the doorway as it's closed again.

We lie in silence for a while until I hear his breathing change. Once Noah's asleep again, I slide from beneath the duvet, knowing any further attempt at rest is futile. In the middle of the double bed, my son looks even smaller than usual, his tiny frame swamped by the thick duvet and Jess's plush, department-store-display pillows.

She was there.

My eyes are drawn to the window, concealed by the floor-length curtains. I think of the layout of Noah's bedroom, the window right by his bed. When he stands on the mattress, he's able to rest his arms on the windowsill to see outside. To see straight into the garden.

The sound of his scream echoes in my head.

She was there.

What if Noah saw far more than any of us realises? Even with our house as remote from others as it is, the moonlight often steals through the gaps in the curtains. Had Noah pulled them open to see outside, that same eerie glow might have been enough to see the shapes of what was happening in the garden.

What if he watched his mother dragging Reka's body to the place where she then buried her?

TWENTY-EIGHT

FRIDAY

On Friday morning, I take Noah to nursery as though nothing has happened. It takes some front to get out of the car in the school car park and walk to the gates of the infants' department as though this is just another normal weekday morning and my wife hasn't been charged with the murder of our nanny whose body was recovered from our back garden. Somehow, I manage it. We don't seem to attract any looks much different to the ones I'm used to us getting, so I wonder whether the news has yet travelled. If it hasn't yet, it will have by the end of today.

'Morning, Noah,' his teacher greets him as we reach the door.

'He hasn't got his uniform, I'm sorry,' I explain. 'We—'

'It's fine,' she answers quickly, barely making eye contact with me. I've only ever met the teacher once before, on parents' evening. I'm usually always in work for drop-off and pick-up times, but she clearly knows who I am. And she knows plenty more than that, too, if the uncomfortable look on her face is anything to go by.

'See you later, mate.' I crouch down to give Noah a hug

before he trudges off to the nursery door carrying his little ruck-sack on his back.

As I leave, I wonder whether I've done the right thing. I'm tempted to run back, tell them I've made a mistake sending him in and I'm taking him home, but then I remember we don't have a home to go to. Instead, I return to the car and call Jonathan, unsure why I'm doing so. He's made the situation as clear as anyone can. Suzanna has confessed to murder. There's little that I or anyone else can do for her now.

'She's refusing to eat,' he tells me.

I rest my head on the steering wheel. I'd feared something like this might happen. Suzanna has always been prone to depression, and there have been occasions I've known her to go days at a time without eating. Sometimes, she'll simply claim to have forgotten.

'Am I allowed to see her yet?'

'It might be permitted, yes. She's considered vulnerable, and she's under review while a place at a holding prison is being—'

'A holding prison? What does that mean?'

'Suzanna will be moved from the station while she awaits sentencing.'

'So, there's no chance of bail?'

Jonathan's silence lasts long enough to answer the question before he needs to. I feel my world come crashing down about me for yet another time. The next time I see Suzanna, it'll either be in a prison visiting room or in a courtroom. Noah won't see his mother for possibly years. He could be a teenager by the time she's released... older, even.

An incoming call interrupts my thoughts. A withheld number.

'I've got a call,' I tell Jonathan. 'I'd better take it.'

I end one call and answer another.

'Mr Cross? It's DI Harris.'

'I've just spoken with our solicitor. He says Suzanna's refusing to eat... is she okay?'

'I'm going to need you to come down to the station.'

I feel my gut twist. I picture Suzanna in a police station cell, a makeshift noose tied around her neck. I see her lying in a hospital bed, her wrists slashed with a piece of broken plastic.

'What's happened? Suzanna—'

'Your wife is fine, Mr Cross. We need to discuss the results of Reka Bako's post-mortem with you.'

'Okay. I can come down now.' Because despite what they think, I have nothing to hide. 'But what's going on?'

'It' s probably better we have this conversation at the station, in person.'

I glance at the clock. 'I'll be there in twenty minutes.'

I get there in less. When I enter the station, I go to reception and let the desk sergeant know I'm there to see DI Harris. A short time later, he appears, and I follow him into the recesses of the station to the kind of interview room I'm already too familiar with. DC Western is already there, waiting for us. There's a file on the table in front of her, closed so I can't see its contents. I'm sure they'll be made known to me soon enough. But it's what's sitting next to it that makes me stop in my tracks. Bagged in clear plastic is a pair of running trainers. The pair Reka wore most days. Next to them, in a separate bag, is her pink raincoat.

'Take a seat.'

I sit without speaking, feeling weightless. When I look at the trainers and coat, I can see Reka wearing them, and I can't seem to tear my eyes from them.

DI Harris starts recording, giving my name, the date and time. 'Do you recognise the items in front of you?'

I nod.

'For the recording, please.'

'Yes,' I say, too sharply. 'Yes, I recognise them.'

'Could you tell us what you see?'

'They're Reka's.' I clear my throat when the words get stuck. 'Reka's trainers. Reka's raincoat.'

'These items weren't in the house when forensics conducted their search on Wednesday,' DI Harris confirms.

'No. I thought she'd taken them... when she'd left.'

Both officers watch me intently, searching for signs of guilt. 'And can you tell us again when you believed Ms Bako to have left your home?'

I think back on the past few days... the past week. 'Tuesday,' I confirm. 'After Noah's accident in the garden. I thought she'd gone without letting us know because she was embarrassed about what had happened and she didn't want to face us.'

Both detectives are silent for a moment. Eventually, it's DC Western who speaks. 'Could you tell us, Mr Cross, how these items came to be in one of your property's outhouses?'

I look from one detective to the other. The outhouses they're referring to are the buildings Suzanna and I had planned to convert into rental holiday homes in the future, once the kids were a bit older and both full time at school. We'd discussed the idea as a retirement investment.

They're watching me, waiting for an answer. I'm about to further incriminate my wife. But I have no choice. I didn't hurt Reka, and if I don't make the police believe that, then I'm going to lose my son. Noah will lose both his parents.

'I don't know.'

'These items were found yesterday,' DI Harris tells me. 'They've already been sent off for testing, and we're awaiting the results.'

'I don't understand.'

'Fingerprints... DNA...'

'But these things might have my fingerprints on them.'

DI Harris raises an eyebrow. 'Ms Bako's trainers? Her

clothes? Why would her personal items have your fingerprints on them?'

I feel myself growing hot, and I know if it shows, it'll look like guilt. 'She was living in our home. Her things were in our house. I might have picked up her trainers to move them... I could have done the same with anything of hers that was left lying around. And Reka was quite slovenly in some ways. She was brilliant with Noah, but when it came to clearing up after herself, we had our issues.' My words are cut short by a recent memory: Suzanna and me standing in the utility room, discussing the wet laundry Reka hadn't taken from the machine. I try to think back on what day that was. Sunday. Reka was already dead.

'Are you okay, Mr Cross? You look pale.'

'I didn't hurt Reka. I told you the last time I saw her or spoke to her, on the driveway on Saturday evening. My wife was watching us from the window, so she'd be able to verify that.' *If she tells the truth*, my brain says.

Which you're not doing, it adds.

DI Harris reaches for the file on the table in front of his colleague. 'We have the results of Ms Bako's post-mortem.'

I feel the blood drain from my face. I'd known this was coming, but whatever is in that file, I don't want to see it. I have visions of photographs, graphic and gruesome, being thrust in front of me against my will: injuries and details I don't want to be exposed to. The memories of being subjected to the findings of Annabelle's post-mortem come back to me, and I feel tears pinching at my eyes. I don't want either of these detectives to see me as vulnerable... yet nor do I want them to regard me as hardened to what happened to Reka.

'A blow to the head consistent with a fall,' DI Harris reads from the paperwork. 'And another,' he adds, looking up at me. 'Blunt force trauma injury to the right-hand side of the skull.'

'I don't understand,' I say, realising how stupid I must sound to them. Either that or arrogant enough to feign ignorance in place of my guilt.

'Ms Bako sustained a small injury after hitting her head on the bathroom door, which matches your wife's account of events. But what she's so far failed to mention was the second and third blows, which the pathologist believes was delivered when Ms Bako was already injured.'

'Third blow?' I repeat, the words not making sense. 'You're saying she was hit after she'd fallen down the stairs?'

The detectives study me impassively, refusing to give anything away. I picture Suzanna at the top of the staircase, looking down on Reka's body. She was alive. She was injured, but she was alive. She could have been helped. Instead, my wife had hit her over the head, finishing off what the fall had failed to achieve.

'Hit with what?' I ask, the words so quiet they're barely audible.

'The pathologist believes the item would have been something heavy. Some kind of household object... an ornament or a lamp.'

I try to think whether anything has been missing from the house, but even if it has, I wouldn't have noticed. The house is no longer of any importance to me: it hasn't been since Annabelle died. For the most part, I've tried to avoid the place, running away from my problems like the coward I've become.

'We're looking into that currently,' DI Harris tells me. 'Do you have any idea what that item might have been?'

'No. I wasn't there, and I don't know. And if Suzanna has confessed, I don't know why she'd withhold information.'

'Neither do we. But we plan to find out.'

I feel a weight fall from me when DI Harris pulls his gaze from me, but the relief is brief. 'There's something else of noticeable interest in the post-mortem report. Skin samples were found beneath Ms Bako's fingernails, suggesting there was a struggle with her attacker before she died. The DNA doesn't match your wife's.'

I feel the floor move beneath me, the chair being moved by an invisible force that threatens to knock me from it.

'We'll need you to provide a sample, Mr Cross. That won't be a problem, will it?'

'No,' I say softly, the word strangled. 'That won't be a problem.'

TWENTY-NINE
FRIDAY

I'm allowed to leave the station, but I'm told not to go too far. I know what the implication is. An arrest could be imminent, and I need to prepare for it. The first thing I do is call Jess to make sure that Noah has been collected from nursery. I hate to ask for her help. I've wanted to talk about what happened that night, but every time I've raised the subject with her, she's struck it dead, like it doesn't matter. And now that she's suggested I may be prone to the same memory lapses as Suzanna, I don't know what to think. It feels as though I'm not sure what's real or not any more.

Either way, I have little other choice than to ask for Jess's help. If anything happens to me – if I end up in custody too – Noah will be taken into care. Once that happens, we may never get him back.

After I've spoken to Jess, I call Jonathan. I update him on what's happened at the station this morning and tell him my DNA sample has been sent off for comparison.

'If you haven't done anything wrong, you don't have anything to worry about,' he tells me, as though it's as simple a case as this.

'What do you mean "if"? I haven't done anything wrong. But we know it doesn't always work like that, does it? Innocent men get sent to prison. And what happens to Noah then, with both his parents in custody?'

'Look, it may not come to this, but are there no family members you can call on to take Noah in for a while?'

'Suzanna's parents are both dead. My mother's in a nursing home. Neither of us has siblings. So, no... there's no family.'

I think of Noah being taken by children's services and put into temporary care, with a family who are strangers to him and know nothing of his history. The thought breaks me. But even more crushing is the notion that perhaps he'd be better off somewhere else, with a family not scarred by grief and trauma.

'If your DNA does come back as a match, you'll be arrested. But it's not necessarily enough for a charge. Reka lived with you... you had regular and easy access to any of her personal belongings. It's circumstantial... it's not enough for a prosecution to find you guilty of murder.'

'But it's a start,' I reply, unable to take any positives from his attempt at reassurance. 'And that's all they need.'

'As soon as you hear anything more from them, you let me know. I'll be straight there, okay?'

I end the call with a feeling of hopelessness, doubtful of Jonathan's ability to get me out of this mess.

When I get back to Jess's house, her car is parked outside. I find her in the kitchen making Noah some lunch, a pile of paperwork stacked on the breakfast bar beside her. Noah is sitting at the dining table with a packet of crayons and a colouring book.

'You okay, mate?' I ask, going over to him and kissing the top of his head. His hair smells stale and in need of washing, and the guilt of neglecting him stabs in my chest. 'How was nursery?'

But he doesn't answer the question, his only response a

slight shrug of his shoulders as he focuses on the picture in front of him.

'I'm so sorry,' I say to Jess, gesturing to the pile of paperwork beside her. 'I'm keeping you from your work.'

'It's fine. Fridays are always my admin days... I don't have any clients. I've cleared my diary for the next week.'

'You shouldn't have done that.'

She turns to flick the switch on the kettle. 'You look terrible.' She reaches for the fruit bowl, grabs an orange and passes it to me. 'You need some vitamin C.'

Her fingers brush mine as I take the fruit, and there's a shock between us.

'Look, Jess, about Saturday...'

Jess glances at Noah. 'You don't need to say anything.'

'No, I do... I do need to.' But even as I speak the words, I'm not sure I even know what I can say. Because I can't remember a thing that happened. Brief snippets of memory here and there, but not the details. And the not-knowing manages to make it all the worse. For the first time, I might have some understanding of what Suzanna is going through.

'You were so tired,' she tells me. 'You've been under so much pressure.'

'I fell asleep?'

She glances again at Noah and nods. 'Don't let him hear this.'

'They're going to arrest me,' I say in barely more than a whisper.

Jess stops what she's doing and looks at me. 'What makes you think that?'

I look at Noah. 'I can't tell you now. But they've found something... something they think links to me.'

She places the butter knife she was using to make sandwiches on the worktop and reaches for my hand before leading me out through the back door and on to the patio. She checks on

Noah before pulling the door to. 'What things?' she asks, her voice lowered.

'Reka's clothes... her trainers. They were in one of the outhouses. When I thought she'd left us, Suzanna must have hidden them there.'

As always, Jess's reaction is calm and unflinching.

'Why do they think you have anything to do with that?'

'I don't know... because Suzanna's accounts of events don't add up? Because they haven't believed me since Wednesday, they've made no secret of that. It's always the husband, isn't it?' I add bitterly.

Jess puts a hand on my arm and lowers her voice to a whisper. 'But you know you didn't hurt Reka.'

'It doesn't matter that I know it. I need them to know it.'

At her forearm, Jess's skin has raised in goosebumps, her T-shirt insufficient against the cold.

'What did you tell the police?' I ask her.

'I already told you. I gave them a history of Suzanna's mental health difficulties... her grief after—'

'I don't mean about Suzanna. I mean about me.'

She meets my eye, and something passes between us, something I don't want to acknowledge or feel. 'Nothing,' she says. 'I didn't say anything about you.'

We're interrupted by Noah, who appears at the door like a tiny pale ghost. I wonder how much he's heard, if anything. 'Come on back in,' I tell him, stepping back into the house. 'It's cold.'

After he's eaten some lunch, I ask Jess if I can take Noah for a bath. It's as much to get away from her as it is to clean his unwashed hair, and as he sits in Jess's bathtub aimlessly drawing circles in the bubbles at his knees, I try to keep myself from thoughts of what's happening back at the station. Because I know what's coming next.

'The water's gone cold,' I say after more time has passed than I'd realised. 'Come on… you'll catch a chill.'

Noah stands in the water, and I pull out the plug before wrapping him in one of Jess's thick towels and carrying him down to her spare bedroom. I take out some of the new clothes she bought him from the supermarket a couple of days ago, and watch while he dresses himself, silently insistent on being independent.

'Noah,' I say to him once he's dressed, and I pat the side of the double bed for him to come and sit beside me. 'There's something I need to tell you, okay? Me and your mum… we might have to go away for a little while. We both love you, you know that, don't you? You'll be safe and looked after, and I might not be gone for lo—'

But already I've made a huge mistake. Noah's face has turned from pale to ghostly white, his grey eyes filled with tears. He looks terrified. I wanted to prepare him, to spare him from the shock of having our absence thrust upon him unexpectedly, yet I've managed to make things so much worse for him than they already were. He must feel as though everyone leaves him: first Annabelle, then Reka, then his mother, now me.

'Noah, come here.'

He falls into my arms, too small to understand what I'm trying to tell him. 'I'm so sorry,' I tell him, gripping him to my chest. 'I love you so, so much.'

And I keep telling him so, repeating it through both our tears until I'm interrupted by the sound of the doorbell. I hear Jess answering it, then a moment later calling my name. I take Noah by the hand, and I tell him that everything's going to be okay, knowing that I'm lying to him. Because some lies are intended to deceive, but others are designed to protect.

When we get to the top of the stairs, DC Western is standing on the doorstep with an officer in uniform.

'Let's not do this here,' I say. 'Please.'

I lead Noah down the stairs, feeling his grip on my hand tighten. When Jess tries to take him away, he resists, clinging to me and sobbing. When I step outside, Jess closes the door quickly, and I walk away to the sound of my son's screams.

'Matthew Cross, I'm arresting you for the murder of Reka Bako. You don't have to say anything, but anything you do say may be later used against you in a court of law.'

She finishes giving me my rights, the words blurred in the whip of wind that catches at my hair. I go silently with them to the waiting car, but before I get into the back seat, DC Western stops me.

'Why did you lie to us about where you were on Saturday evening?'

PART THREE

SUZANNA

THIRTY

SATURDAY

Jonathan hurries me from the court building once we leave the bail hearing. I'm grateful for the terrible weather. A huddle of people who I assume are press are gathered at the bottom of the steps, trying to shelter beneath umbrellas that are being bent by the force of the wind. By the time they spot us leaving, we already have our backs to them, heading towards his car parked in the next side street.

I hear someone call my name, but Jonathan puts a hand on my shoulder, pressing me onwards. He doesn't talk to me until we're in the car and have started moving.

'You understand the bail conditions?'

I shiver beneath my soaked jacket, the thin fabric inadequate for the conditions.

'Yes.' I'm not to go further than five miles from where I'll be staying, which until we're able to return home, I assume will be Jess's house. I know that's where Matthew and Noah have been staying, though Matthew might suggest that with the three of us together again we'd be better at a hotel. Wherever we end up, I won't want to leave there. Even had the five-mile rule not been imposed by the court, it's one I would have chosen for myself. I don't want to go anywhere or be seen. If it was just me, I'd never need to leave the house again. But I know at some point I'll need to face the outside world again, for Noah.

'I don't understand why they've let me go.'

'They don't believe you were responsible for Reka's death, only her unlawful burial. You're not a risk to the public, Suzanna. So long as you don't break the terms of your bail, you'll be free until sentencing.'

So much was said during the hearing. My mental health was picked apart as though I wasn't sitting there right in front of those people. Text messages I'd sent to Reka after the night of her death were read aloud – one asking her not to join us at dinner on Sunday night, others saying that we needed to talk. The trauma of Annabelle's death was discussed in so much detail that I had to switch myself off from it.

A second, unspoken conclusion was made: I may not be dangerous, but I'm still out of my mind.

I know I'm still facing prison. I don't know whether I'll survive it, though I know it's what I deserve.

Last night, I'd screamed out in my sleep. There'd been banging on the wall, someone from the next cell along yelling at me to shut the fuck up. In my nightmare, I'd seen myself as though I was floating above my own body. I was at the bottom of the staircase with Reka at my feet. She wasn't moving. I was shaking... panicked. I could see my body shuddering with shock as I looked helplessly from above, willing myself to do some-thing – anything – other than what I knew would come next.

'I didn't kill her.'

Jonathan glances at me as he pulls off from a set of traffic lights. I see the reaction that flickers behind his eyes; I'm not sure he believes me, despite the police now seeming to. He's known Matthew for years... he's been lumbered with me by association.

'I thought I had. I mean, I must have, mustn't I... that's how it seemed. I get these blackouts... I don't remember what happened. But I took her to the garden, I know that much was real.'

I'm saying too much. Jonathan looks uncomfortable in the face of my admissions now they're being made beyond the secure settings of a police station and the courtroom. His face is pinched and restrained. He's holding something back.

'But if they don't think I killed her...'

'They've arrested Matthew.'

I smile like an idiot, his words sounding foreign. 'They can't have. I mean... someone would have said something, wouldn't they?'

I can't decipher Jonathan's expression. Either he thinks me an idiot or a liar... I can't be sure which.

'Matthew didn't hurt Reka. He wouldn't. He wasn't even there.'

'Let's wait to see what unfolds today,' he says, as though we're waiting for the next episode of a three-part drama, and this isn't my family on the brink of ruin.

He takes a left turn, and we pass a primary school. The playground is deserted, its climbing frames and wooden ship abandoned to the terrible weather.

'Who's Noah with?' I ask, assuming he must be with Jess. Jonathan confirms the fact. I can't begin to imagine what effect this past week must have had on him. And now I'm going to have to offer some sort of explanation as to where his father is.

'Matthew couldn't have hurt Reka. He was out on Saturday night... he didn't get home until late Sunday morning.'

'He lied to the police, Suzanna. He told them he was at the charity event all evening on Saturday, but he wasn't. The organisers said he never arrived, that he called last minute and said there'd been a family emergency. There was plenty enough time for him to have got home.'

I picture Matthew and me standing in the utility room,

talking about the event. The way he'd so casually responded when I'd asked him about how it went. I'd naïvely thought it had been difficult for him, an event he hadn't wanted to attend but had bravely endured. Instead, he'd lied to my face.

'They've made a mistake.'

'There's no mistake, Suzanna. He was never there.' Jonathan's face softens slightly. 'And I'm sorry... but there's more.'

Jonathan starts to give me the details: Reka's clothing... skin cells... DNA. His words float over me as though I'm in a bubble, listening to him from a space that can't be reached.

Reka. I'd known there was something going on... I'd felt it in my gut. I'd seen the way she looked at him... the way he looked at her. Had she tried to break things off between them? Had she threatened to tell me, and he reacted by shoving her? It might have been an accident. But he kept the secret to himself, just like I did. He let me take the blame for what he'd done.

'Skin cells beneath her fingernails?' I repeat, clutching at some of the details he has offered me.

'There must have been a struggle... Reka tried to defend herself.'

My chest swells with pain. For Reka. For Noah. For the lies that Matthew and I have told, each with our own reasons. The secrets we've kept from each other.

Neither of us speaks for the rest of the journey. When we arrive at Jess's house, I unclip my seat belt, but I'm hesitant about moving from the car. Noah has no reason to trust me any more. I have no idea what Matthew has told him, and therefore no idea what I should say. Our stories won't align, and it'll give our son greater reason to doubt both of us. One day, when he's older, he'll be able to look at our history for himself, our family's story documented with a few quick internet searches. There'll be no more hiding. No more lying.

One day, when he's older, we're going to have to tell Noah the truth.

THIRTY-ONE
SATURDAY

When I see my son sitting on Jess's sofa, I go to put my arms around him. But he recoils from me as though I'm a stranger. From where she stands in the doorway, I see Jess's reaction. I wonder how much Noah has overheard of the conversations that have taken place since my arrest on Wednesday. Does he know what happened to Reka? Does he know what everyone, including me, has thought me guilty of?

'I missed you so much,' I tell him.

There's a twitch at his cheek, a tiny flicker of a reaction. It's a small gesture, but I cling gratefully to it all the same. I sit beside him, stretch my hand towards him, there should he want to take it. But for now, he doesn't.

'Thank you for looking after him.'

Jess meets my eyes sadly, sympathy stamped across her tired face. I'd underestimated how much of an impact this would have had on her too. In my absence, she's been looking after Matthew as well as Noah.

'There must be a mistake. Matthew would ne—'

But Jess shakes her head, rightly shutting me down. We can't have this conversation in front of Noah.

'Would you like to watch some TV?' Jess asks him. She searches for the remote and finds a cartoon channel. Noah curls himself into the far corner of the sofa, seeming already so familiar with the place. My heart cracks a little at the notion that he seems more comfortable here with her than he does in his own home – or, at least, what was once his home. We're never going to be able to live there again now, not after everything that's happened. I've no idea where we'll go, or even how much longer we'll have together, but for now all I can think about is Matthew being in custody.

'I'm sorry,' Jess apologises, 'he's been watching far too much TV. I don't really have much here to keep a child entertained.'

'Don't apologise. You've done more than anyone should have asked of you.'

'I offered. And I'm sorry I wasn't there today. I wanted to be, but...' She doesn't finish her sentence, but she looks at Noah and I understand. There was no one else to look after him. After Annabelle's death, we were cut adrift.

Jess rests the remote on the arm of the sofa by Noah. 'Shall I get you something to eat?' she offers him.

He looks to me as though for confirmation he's allowed to have something before he nods.

'Has he spoken at all since he's been here?' I ask as I follow Jess down to the kitchen.

'Not to me. But I think he's spoken to Matthew. He's been having nightmares... I've heard him shouting out at night.'

I wonder what Matthew has told him about Reka. I wonder what he's said about me.

'Does he like pizza?' Jess asks, opening the freezer.

'Yes. Thank you. Do you know when they're going to let us go back to the house? I don't have any of my things.'

'I don't know. Matthew said it's still being treated as a crime scene. And now they've found Reka's things—'

'They said his DNA was under her fingernails. That she must have put up a fight before she died.' My words choke on a sob, and Jess stops what she's doing.

She puts the plastic-wrapped frozen pizza on the breakfast bar and comes over to me. She puts her hands on my shoulders and looks at me intently. 'Take a deep breath,' she instructs me. 'You're okay.'

I think about that night again, the shapes and colours of it merging into a picture that has started to look clearer since I've been in custody. I knocked into Reka after we'd argued, I know that much to be true. I was upset... not thinking straight. Then I remember being in bed with Noah, curling myself against his body with the fear that Matthew and Reka might have been plotting to take him away from me. That much might still have been true. Maybe one of them had changed their mind. Matthew needed to silence her, to make sure I never found out what they'd been doing.

No, I can't believe it. I won't believe it.

'I didn't do it,' I tell her through tears. 'I thought it must have been me... but I know now that it wasn't.'

As I cry, Jess holds me. She doesn't try to rush me or tell me to stop, just allowing me to stand here and feel the release that crying brings with it, because over this past week I feel as though I've been holding my breath, waiting for someone to give me permission to breathe. I had hoped that person would be Matthew. Now, I'm not even sure I ever knew him.

'None of this is your fault,' Jess tells me.

'I may not have killed Reka, but I still buried her. It was a terrible, awful thing to do.'

'Your behaviour was manipulated by the medication.'

I inhale deeply, trying to calm my stuttered speech. 'I think Matthew's been overmedicating me. It would have been so easy for him to do... I never noticed anything. That day last week when you challenged him about my meds... no wonder he reacted so defensively. He knew you were suspicious of him.'

Jess lets me go and walks over to the sink. She takes a clean glass from the draining board and fills it with water, gulping nearly all of it in one go.

'The police realise all this. They wouldn't have let you go otherwise. By the time you go for sentencing, everything will be out in the open. He won't get away with it.'

'But why would he do that to me? I thought he wanted to help me get better. Ever since Annabelle...'

But I can still barely bring myself to speak the words. Jess tears the plastic from the pizza and slides it on to an oven tray. 'We don't have the answers to everything yet. Perhaps Matthew was the one who should have been psychoanalysed. Perhaps he might also get an assessment in custody.'

I watch her take the tray to the oven and slide it on to the middle shelf before going back to the fridge and taking out a cucumber and a packet of cherry tomatoes. She takes them to the chopping board and pulls a knife from the wooden block that rests beside the microwave.

'Why didn't you tell me that Matthew never turned up to the charity evening on Saturday?'

Jess stops what she's doing, the knife held poised in her hand. She can't bring herself to look at me.

'Jess. Please. If you knew he wasn't there, why haven't you said anything?'

It had never crossed my mind until now. There'd been no reason for it to, because as far as I'd been aware, Jess and Matthew had been to that event together. He'd asked her to go because I hadn't wanted to, and now I can't help the feeling that if I'd just said yes and faced my fears, none of this would be happening. Reka would still be alive.

But Jess has known all this time that he wasn't ever there. And for whatever reason, she's kept that knowledge hidden, from me and from the police. She's my best friend. I never thought she would lie to me, and never about something as big as this.

Jess puts the knife down on the chopping board, finally raising her head to make eye contact with me. 'He was here,' she says. 'He was with me.'

THIRTY-TWO

SATURDAY

'I can explain everything,' Jess tells me. 'And I promise you, it isn't how it sounds. Will you let me make Noah's lunch first? We can talk properly then.'

I sit at the dining table, shock rendering me useless. I think of the way that Jess and Matthew behaved around each other on the morning she challenged him over my medication, and I realise now how naïve I've been. Their exchange was positively hostile. Guilt? Shame? I'd thought I was the cause of the awkwardness between them, but maybe I was further from the truth than I could possibly have imagined. The worst assumptions fill my mind. I thought he'd been having an affair with Reka. Perhaps I was suspicious of the wrong woman for all this time.

Jess doesn't speak again as she prepares Noah some vegetable slices and waits to take the pizza from the oven. She asks me if I'd like a slice as though nothing has happened, as though she hasn't just told me that my husband spent the evening with her and they both then lied to me about it afterwards. I take the plate from her when she moves for the door, not wanting her to see Noah again until we've had a chance to talk. I expect her to object, but she doesn't.

When I get to the living room, I see Noah has fallen asleep on the sofa. There's a blanket hanging from one of the arms, so I take it and cover him, planting a kiss on his forehead before quietly telling him that I love him. Whatever really happened on Saturday, it doesn't seem to matter now. Noah needs to be my focus, and I know I'm guilty of having neglected my responsibility towards him.

I delay going back to the kitchen for as long as I can get away with, part of me not wanting to have to face what awaits me there. But I need to hear the truth. The missing pieces of Saturday evening are in someone else's possession, and until I'm able to see them for what they truly are, I'll never be able to make sense of my own involvement in what happened to Reka.

When I get back to the kitchen, Jess is sitting at the dining table. There's a cup of tea in front of her and a second waiting beside it, for me.

'If he was here with you on Saturday night, you need to tell the police. He has an alibi. He can't have killed Reka.'

'It isn't that straightforward.'

'What do you mean? Why not?'

'I didn't know how to tell you,' she says as I sit down. 'I was waiting for a right time, but there was never going to be one. And then you were arrested.'

I flinch at her words. 'Just tell me. How long has it been going on?'

Jess's eyes narrow. 'What do you mean?'

'You and Matthew,' I say, forcing myself to remain calm in the face of her feigned ignorance. 'How long?'

'There is no me and Matthew. I would never do that to you.'

And despite what she's just told me, I believe her. Jess has been with me through my entire adult life. She's been the first

190   VICTORIA JENKINS

to cheer me on at every success and the first shoulder to cry on at every failure. She would never betray me with my husband.

Yet she's already lied, a voice inside my head reminds me.

'So what happened on Saturday?' I ask, confused.

'I'd just got out of the shower. I was up in the bedroom, about to start getting ready for the event, when there was a loud noise from downstairs. Glass being smashed. I panicked. My phone was on the bedside table. I didn't know whether there was someone in the house, but I was certain a window had been broken. I didn't know what to do. I called Matthew.'

'You didn't think to call the police?' I ask, unable to keep the sarcasm from my tone.

'Of course I did. But I couldn't. Please... let me explain. I stayed upstairs in the bedroom with the dressing table pulled across the door until my phone rang and Matthew told me he was outside. He went around the back to check there was no one there, and when he reassured me that the place was empty, I went downstairs to let him in. The kitchen window had been smashed... There was a brick on the floor by the oven.'

'Why would someone throw a brick through the window and then not come in to take anything?'

'I don't know. There must have been a noise or something from one of the neighbours. Whoever it was, they were disturbed... they must have run off before anyone saw them.'

'So Matthew turns up all suited like a hero.' I picture him as he'd looked in his suit that evening; then I see Jess, straight out of the shower, still wrapped in just a towel when meeting him at the door. Her hair and skin still wet. 'And then what?'

'Suzanna, I know what you're thinking. But it wasn't like that.' She closes her eyes and presses her fingertips to her forehead. 'I woke up naked in my bed,' she says, unable to look me in the eye. 'The following morning. There were marks on my thighs. There was—' But her words catch in her throat, and she can't bring herself to tell me any further details. 'I had no idea what time it was, but I could sense it was the early hours of the morning. I couldn't remember anything at first, and then tiny snippets of memory started coming back, distorted. He'd been insistent that I eat something, I remember that. He told me I looked pale... that my blood sugar must have been low. He seemed so concerned. There was some leftover lasagne in the fridge. I let him take it out and heat it in the microwave. He took a slice for himself, but when I thought about it afterwards, I couldn't remember seeing him eat any of it. He kept trying to persuade me to call the police, to report the attempted break-in. I didn't want to because I knew what a waste of time it would have been. When I was a teenager, someone broke into my parents' house. I was home alone at the time, and I was attacked and robbed... I was put through all kinds of examinations after-wards. The police made me feel like it was my fault, like I'd somehow been asking for it. They questioned whether I'd been drinking... what I'd been wearing. They managed to make me feel worse than the attacker had. It was like being assaulted a second time around. I couldn't face going through any of it again.'

'You've never told me this before.'

'I never wanted to think about that night again. And that's why I didn't want to tell Matthew any of it either. Anyway, we were talking, and he was trying to calm me down... and then I don't know. I don't remember going upstairs. I don't remember anything. I just woke up and it was morning, and I had a terrible headache, worse than any hangover I've ever had.'

'You're saying he drugged your food?'

I think again of the exchange between Matthew and Jess that I'd walked in on last week, when Matthew had reacted angrily to Jess's suggestion that I had somehow been overmed-icated. She'd been about to expose him, and he'd reacted like a guilty man.

'Do you think he... on Saturday...?'

But I can't bring myself to say the words. I think of the way he was with me on the night of Noah's accident, his hands around my throat, his body forced against mine. I hadn't recognised my own husband. I had thought him angry at Reka, that perhaps his response to me was a reaction to whatever had happened between them. But it all looks so different now, the memory of that night altered by what Jess now claims he'd done to her less than two days earlier.

When I look at her, there are tears in her eyes. I don't want to believe it. Yet doubt has crept beneath my skin, insidious and toxic.

'Why didn't you tell me? Or report him?' I take her hand in mine and squeeze her fingers.

'And do that to you? How could I put you through that when you were already going through so much?'

I can't believe it, because I don't want to. 'How could you have had him here, living in your house? If he'd...'

It doesn't make sense. Surely Jess wouldn't have been able to stand having him in her home these past few days if she truly believed him guilty of drugging and assaulting her.

'What would have happened to Noah?' she says, seeming to read my doubts. 'If I'd reported Matthew while you were in custody, Noah would have been taken into care. I had to wait until you were released. I could never forgive myself if you had Noah taken from you too.'

I hang my head, ashamed that my grief has forced Jess to conceal her own. That she has silenced her own suffering to protect me from further pain. And yet, I suppose, this is what true friends do for each other.

'I'm sorry,' I say quietly.

'This isn't your fault, Suzanna.'

'I still buried Reka's body. I should have gone for help... I should have told someone.'

'You acted in fear,' Jess says. 'You were frightened you'd lose another child. I understand it. The courts have understood that too – they wouldn't have let you out on bail if they didn't. But you see now why I can't help Matthew, don't you? I can't give him an alibi. He made sure I was out of it on Saturday night. After that, he could have been anywhere.'

We fall into an awful silence, together, but alone with our separate thoughts. All this time I've leaned on Matthew for support, knowing his grief must be as intense as mine. Yet all this time, I've been married to a liar. A murderer. By Jess's account... a rapist.

THIRTY-THREE

SUNDAY

So much makes sense now. The more hours that had passed in custody, the more my thoughts seemed to achieve a kind of clarity, that just by being alone without the distractions of my life, I was beginning to see things as they really were, and not as I had tried to create them. Noah lies beside me, snoring gently. He still hasn't been able to bring himself to hug me, but that's okay. I don't want to push him. I need to earn his trust. I need to prove myself to him, that we might start to get to know each other all over again. Hopefully then, by the time he's old enough to find out for himself what happened to Reka, he'll understand why I did what I did. I'd already had my daughter taken away from me. I would have done anything not to lose my son.

I reach to the bedside table and press my phone to light the screen: 2.36 a.m. That time of night when all the bad things gather around the bed, appearing bigger than they really are. But surely bigger now means clearer. The closer they are, the better I'm able to make out the details.

I didn't kill Reka. I know that now, with as much certainty as I know the time of night and the colour of the duvet cover that I lie beneath. I'm also now sure of something else: my treatment was making me worse, not better. I don't know what Matthew had been giving me, or whether he'd simply been increasing my dosages; either way, our whole situation has started to look far different in the days since I've been without the drugs. The medication that I'd believed to be helping me was the very thing that had been distorting my ability to see things as they really were. Rather than suffer with the effects of withdrawal, the absence of those drugs was clearing my mind, like a plough driving through a snowdrift, allowing me to see what lies ahead. Allowing me to see what lay behind, too.

I didn't kill Reka, and I told myself this, over and over, making myself believe it. In much the same way I had managed to convince myself of my guilt. After making my initial confession at the police station, I sat alone in a cell and went over what I'd told the officers in my statement. Reka and I had argued. I'd pushed her. She'd fallen down the stairs. Yet later, a little over an hour after I'd given my statement, I said something different, they later claimed. There'd been a gap between the incidents: between Reka and me arguing and her falling down the stairs. They'd asked me how much time had passed between those two things, but I couldn't tell them. And I could see what they were beginning to think: that if I couldn't be sure of that information, how could I be certain of anything else?

I realise now what they must have suspected: that I confessed to protect someone else. My husband. I presume that's why no one told me of his arrest until after my bail terms had been agreed.

It makes sense that while living with us, Reka might have been able to see something in Matthew that I'd missed. I had trusted him implicitly... I'd never had a reason not to. But she came into our home as an outsider, and without the familiarity of a prior relationship she would have been able to see things I hadn't, despite them being right in front of me. Sometimes, the most obvious facts are the ones we refuse to acknowledge.

Perhaps there was never an affair. Or maybe there was, and getting closer to Matthew enabled Reka a greater insight into his manipulation of my 'recovery'. Maybe he forced himself on her as he did with Jess. There's a chance she realised what he'd been doing to me, and perhaps she threatened to expose his secret. Maybe he needed to silence her before she had the chance.

My head begins to hurt with the intensity of my thoughts. At some point, I drift into sleep and back out again, in and out, pulled amid broken snatches of sleep.

There's a noise along the landing, the creak of a door. I think at first that it's Jess going to the bathroom, but after a while, when she still hasn't left to return to her bedroom, I sit up in bed, listening carefully for any sound. And that's when I realise that Noah is no longer beside me.

I slide quietly from the bed and go to the bedroom door, gently easing it open. The bathroom light has been left on so that Noah might find his way if he were to wake up in the night. But when I get to the opened door, he isn't there. At the end of the corridor, Jess's bedroom door is shut. I turn to go back along the landing, and that's when I hear a noise from downstairs.

My heart thunders as I grip the banister and slowly make my way down the staircase, careful not to make a sound. I want to call Noah's name, to hear him shout back to me, but if there's someone with him, I don't want to alarm them, and I know that Noah won't call out to me anyway. I'm nearly at the bottom of the staircase when I notice the door to Jess's office is open. It's a small room at the front of the house, just big enough for a computer desk, a chair and a filing cabinet. The light is off, but when I go inside, I almost cry out in fright at the sight of Noah sitting there in the darkness. On the desk in front of him, pressed beneath his little palm, is a photograph. In the half-light, I'm unable to make out what it shows. But then I move closer, and the photograph becomes illuminated by the light from the streetlamp that filters through the half-closed curtains.

Me.

I recognise the image. A journalist took the photograph moments after Matthew and I had left the coroner's court following the inquest into Annabelle's death. I look grey in the photograph, my cheeks sunken and my eyes shadowed with dark circles. I remember so little about that day. I left that building as though in a nightmare, looking down upon myself like I was removed from my body, and I continued to live that way, not bothering to try to convince even myself that I could be anything other than broken.

'Noah,' I say softly. 'It's okay. Come back upstairs to bed.'

But my heart is pounding in my chest, and I need to see what lies beneath the photograph. I crouch down in front of my son, my eyes catching his in the half-light.

'Can I see? Where did you find these?'

He points to the drawer in the desk.

'Okay. Let's just put them back then, shall we? They're not ours, are they?'

I gently move his hand away from the pile, managing to push the photograph of myself aside as I do. Beneath it, there's an article from a local newspaper relating to the circumstances of Annabelle's death. Then another, this one focused on Matthew and his fundraising endeavours. I pick the pile up quickly, expecting Noah to object. When he doesn't, I flit through them hastily, seeing piece after piece of our lives slip through my fingers.

I pull open the drawer Noah had pointed to, finding it now empty. Beneath it, there's a second. But when I pull on the handle, it doesn't budge. It's locked.

'Suzanna. Is everything okay?'

I stop what I'm doing, letting the photographs and clippings fall back to the sofa. Noah looks down between his knees, his focus kept on the carpet.

I turn to Jess, who appears as a silhouette in the office doorway.

'What's all this?' I ask her.

THIRTY-FOUR

SUNDAY

With Noah back in bed, I go downstairs and into the kitchen, where Jess is waiting for me. In front of her is the pile of papers and photographs Noah took from the office drawer. My family's history, condensed to a collection of reports.

'It's all my fault, Suzanna,' she says, not giving me a chance to speak. 'I built a profile of you and your family, to help you. It's my job as a therapist to know my patients in as much detail as possible, and although we've been friends all these years, what you've been through this past year changed everything. I wanted to try to understand, so I could help you heal. But while I was wrapped up in my focus on you, I managed to overlook just how much psychiatric help Matthew might have needed. If I'd paid him more attention, perhaps we wouldn't be here now. I'm so sorry. I've let you down.'

I sit opposite her, keeping a distance, hating the effect that all this is having on me.

'It looks a bit obsessive,' I point out.

She sighs. 'You're my friend. My best friend. You know what I'm like with my work. I suppose it's always been a kind of obsession.' She leans across and takes my hand in hers. 'You've always been so good to me. It's my duty to look after you. When we first met at uni, I saw something in you then. Something that was broken, long before Matthew was even in the picture. Something I was confident I could fix. That's what I do... what I aim to do, at least.'

'I'm not a project, Jess.'

'No... God... I didn't mean that at all. I have so much respect for you, Suzanna. More than you probably realise. You're a brilliant woman, successful and talented. And I'll admit... I've always been fascinated by your mind. You're a mass of contradictions... we've spoken about that in the past. You're confident yet insecure. Successful yet unfulfilled. If I was going to be able to help you, I needed to understand as much as I could about what this past year must have been like for you.'

'Did you need therapy, after the attack?'

'What attack?'

'When you were a teenager.'

'Oh God, yes. I mean, I needed it, but I never got it. I didn't dare to... I was too scared to talk through what had happened all over again. I kept everything to myself. And I know that's what you've been tempted to do too. I know why you feel you could never talk to anyone else about what's going on inside your head. But I've seen the results of how damaging it can be, to keep everything withheld like that, and I've never wanted anyone else to go through what I had to... to feel that alone.'

In all the years I've known her, I don't think I've ever once regarded Jess as vulnerable in any way. She is the confident, capable one: assertive and self-assured. She's always taken a lead in social situations, and if I'm honest, I've always wondered why it wasn't Jess that Matthew had been drawn to on the night we'd all first met. For whatever reason, he had wanted me, and I suppose, in those early days at least, I'd felt a gratitude for it, that someone as good-looking and successful as Matthew had wanted to spend time with and get to know me. And maybe there was a reason for that.

'I never knew you felt this way,' I admit. 'I'm sorry that I wasn't there for you.'

She reaches across the table and takes my hand in hers. 'You've always been there for me. You're the only person who's ever been consistent in my life.'

'But if I'd known about—'

'That doesn't matter. It was my decision for you not to know.' She pulls her hand away and sits back. 'Everything's going to be okay, I promise. Look... I was thinking. We should get away for a few days, me, you and Noah. I already cleared my schedule, in case I was needed to look after Noah. My mother's got a little flat near the coast in Dorset – it's only a two-bed but plenty enough space for the three of us. The break would do you good.'

'My bail conditions,' I remind her. 'I'm not allowed to go outside a five-mile radius of this place.'

She sighs. 'Of course. I'm sorry... I wasn't thinking. When all this is over then, what do you think?'

I give a vague nod of agreement – anything to get a change of subject. Jess seems to be forgetting that I may still be sent to prison for the unlawful burial of Reka's body. She's speaking as though this will one day be over, which for me it never will. I will live with what I did every day.

'You mustn't feel that everything has been a lie.'

I meet her eye. 'What do you mean?' I ask, not knowing exactly what she's referring to.

'Matthew. What he did to me.'

I look down at my hands. I still don't want to believe it, but there's a part of me that does, and I just can't help it. What happened last week... the way he was with me. I'd never known him to be like that before.

'I'd only known him a couple of years before I got pregnant

with Noah. I suppose it isn't enough time to really know a person.'

'You mustn't blame yourself, either.' She comes over to me, sits beside me. She takes my hand in hers, closing her cold fingers around my own.

'I don't want you to look back at your marriage and feel like everything was a lie.'

'But that's what it has been.'

'No. This isn't your fault. You trusted him and he took advantage of you. You're a good woman, Suzanna. A good person. Matthew doesn't deserve you. He never did.' She lets go of my hand. 'I'm going to head back up. Give me a shout if you need anything, okay?'

When she goes back up to bed, I do the same, but I find myself unable to sleep. I keep thinking about the locked drawer in her office, and now I wish I'd asked her about it while I'd had the chance. If there are 'profiles' of her other clients in that drawer, why are they kept locked when mine was so accessible that Noah was able to get his hands on it? Perhaps she'd only recently been looking through something she'd thought relevant, and that's why the first drawer had been unlocked.

Just ask her tomorrow, I tell myself, but I know that in the morning, in the stark light of day, it's going to be harder to do so.

Eventually, I go back downstairs. I make myself a coffee and I sit in the kitchen scrolling my phone, searching for things relating to Reka and Matthew. I remember him on the driveway with her on the evening he never made it to the charity fundraiser. The following day, how he spoke to me about it, claiming to have hardly seen Jess while they were there. I had thought my husband many things, but never a liar.

Second arrest in nanny murder, one headline on my screen reads.

Police shift focus as Bako family arrive in UK, screams another.

Oh God, I think, my heart dropping in my chest. Reka's family are here. They'll want answers that nobody seems able to offer. Not yet, at least.

I think of Reka's mother – her *anya* – picturing her face as I'd seen it in the photo montage that was pinned to the cork-board in Reka's bedroom. I imagine her heartbreak, recognising it as my own. I know what it is to lose a child. I feel her grief now, reliving the pain all over again.

Only, Annabelle's death was a tragic accident. Reka was murdered, her life stolen from her in a moment of intentional violence. Because she didn't die as I thought she had, from a fall down the stairs.

I start at the sound of my phone ringing. Jonathan.

'Hello,' I answer quickly, hoping the call hasn't disturbed either Noah or Jess. I move to the back door for a clearer signal.

'Suzanna. I'm sorry to call so early. There's been an update, and I didn't think it should wait. Where are you?'

'Jess's house. We still can't go home yet. Do you know how much longer it's going to be before we can—'

'You and Noah are both at Jess's house now?'

'Yes. Jonathan... what is it? What's happened?'

'Okay. Look, I'm going to come and pick you up. I'll be twenty minutes.'

My heart stutters at the change in tone of his voice. 'Please just tell me what's going on.'

'Reka's call records have been released to the police. The last call she received on Saturday night was from Jess. There were texts between them... the last one sent from Reka that afternoon.'

'Okay,' I say, trying to keep myself calm... trying not to jump to conclusions. 'What did it say?'

'"I know what you've done."'

My skin turns to ice.

'Get Noah and keep your phone with you,' Jonathan tells

me. 'Leave the house as soon as you can and call me when you're outside. Don't worry about getting anything else from there.'

Jonathan ends the call, and I'm left feeling more terrified than I've ever felt. I shove my mobile into the waistband of Jess's borrowed pyjama trousers and head upstairs to the spare bedroom, wondering how I'm going to get Noah up and out of the house without alerting Jess to the fact. For the first time since he fell into silence, I find myself grateful for it. At least I know I won't have to worry about any noise, other than my own.

There must be a mistake, I think. *I know what you've done.* That could refer to anything. Perhaps Reka had suspected there was something going on between Matthew and Jess, in the same way I'd mistakenly believed him to be involved with Reka. She might have thought herself showing loyalty to me by confronting Jess about it, and maybe Jess's call had been an attempt to put straight her suspicions.

Yet something doesn't sit right. I can't tear my thoughts away from those photographs and clippings that Noah had been sitting with. How had he known where to find them? And what the hell is in that locked drawer?

The urgency in Jonathan's voice implied danger, and I can't shake the thought of it as I move stealthily along the landing, like a thief adept at silence. The door to the spare bedroom is ajar, and I slip into the room soundlessly. The duvet is crumpled in a pile at my side of the bed, still pushed back from where I left it. On the other side of the bed, Noah's pillow shows the indentation of where his little head had lain.

But Noah isn't here.

THIRTY-FIVE

SUNDAY

It is moments later, back out on the landing, that I hear it.

'La la lu... la la lu.'

I'm catapulted back to that afternoon in the park, searching for Noah before hearing those haunting lyrics in the foreign sound of his small voice. But this time, it's not his voice I hear. It's Jess's. I hurry along the landing and burst into her room. She's sitting on the edge of her bed, with Noah lying beside her. He's curled on top of her duvet, still asleep.

'What are you doing?'

'He was crying,' she says. 'I didn't want you to be disturbed.'

There is another explanation, I try to tell myself. Whatever Reka was referring to in that text, it was something innocent. Innocuous. I step towards the bed, ready to take my son back to our room. But Jess stands, blocking him from me.

'What are you doing?' I ask again.

I wonder whether she heard me talking to Jonathan downstairs. She would only have caught my side of the conversation, and now I wrack my brain trying to think of its details, unable to recollect what's just happened no more than a couple of minutes ago.

'You need to sleep, Suzanna. You look exhausted.'

'I'm fine. I just want to take Noah back to the other room.'

'But he's sleeping now. If you wake him, he'll be distressed again. Why would you want to disturb him when he's sleeping so peacefully?'

I don't know what to do. If I tell Jess now about Reka's phone records, I've no idea how she might react. Jonathan will be here soon, and if I'm not outside waiting for him with Noah, he's going to come in the house.

'I just want to take my son,' I say, trying to keep the words from wobbling with the fear that's resting in my gut.

'I don't think that's a good idea.'

Her words cut through the air between us.

'He's my son.'

'But you're not coping, Suzanna. You know that, deep down.'

It's now that I notice the glass on the bedside table, half filled with water. Half empty. I look again at Noah, sleeping too soundly. Our arguing should have woken him up. Yet he's slept right through it.

'What have you given him?'

'Just something to let him sleep.'

'He's just a child,' I say, my voice rising as I fight to stay calm.

'He'll be fine. It's just to give you some space and time. That's all you've ever really needed.'

'What I need,' I tell her, gritting my teeth, 'is the truth. That's all I've ever really needed.'

'And you know you'll always get that from me.'

'So why didn't you tell me you'd called Reka on the night she died?'

Behind Jess's eyes, a succession of thoughts passes in a blur of muted light. 'I didn't.'

But she's lying. I know she's lying, and I can see in her face that she realises it too. Earlier, it had occurred to me that I'd never seen Jess vulnerable before. Perhaps there's a good reason for it. She isn't vulnerable. She is confident. Capable. Self-assured.

She always knows exactly what she's doing.

'Oh my God,' I say, my eyes flitting again to Noah, who still hasn't stirred. 'Matthew didn't kill Reka.'

'I know you don't want to believe him guilty. But the police have evidence, Suzanna. His DNA was beneath her finger-nails... you told me so yourself.'

'No. The phone records, Jess... you called her on the night she died. How could you have done that if you'd been drugged by Matthew, like you told me?'

Hadn't that been what she'd said? That she couldn't give Matthew an alibi because he'd made sure she was out of it.

She steps towards me and I back away. 'Don't you see what he's done?' she says. 'What he's doing? He's still managing to manipulate you, even now when he's in custody. He must have taken my phone after I was unconscious. He called Reka from my number, then he went home, and he killed her. She must have realised what he'd been doing to you... she was close enough living in your home to see what was really going on. The police will realise that's what happened. They can see him for what he is. Why can you still not see it?'

My head hurts with confusion. A thousand memories come flooding back: the days the children were born... our wedding day... the morning he lay with me on the bathroom floor when I was too grief-stricken to move. People are capable of being more than one thing: good and bad. But not Matthew. Not this.

I doubted him, but I was wrong. I may have known Jess longer, but I realise now that I have no idea of what she is capable of.

'You had her bracelet... the one she always wore. It was broken. Did you keep it as some sort of souvenir?'

'I told you,' she says flatly. 'I found it by the sugar pot.'

But she is lying, just like she's lied about everything else. I would have noticed it there at some point, before she'd shown it to me.

'What's in the drawer downstairs, Jess?'

'What drawer?'

'The second drawer in your office desk. The one you keep locked. What's in there?'

Jess sighs and her face changes. She looks at me sympatheti-cally, almost pityingly, as she has done so many times before during our sessions. Yet I see it differently now. I don't want her pity. And now I feel certain I should never have asked for her help.

'My accounts,' she says. 'I'll take you down there and show you, if you like? It's all very boring.'

She moves to the door as though expecting me to follow her, but I'm not leaving this room without my son. When I make a move towards Noah, Jess grabs me by the arm, yanking me back sharply. Her other hand moves deftly to her pocket, and she pulls out a syringe.

'There's enough in here to make sure Noah never wakes again. I don't want to do it, Suzanna, so please don't make me. But I promise you, if you try to take him from this room, I'll do it. And there'll be no coming back from it.'

I look at the syringe in her hand, and everything comes crashing on top of me. All this time, it's been Jess who's kept me medicated. Jess manipulating me. Jess keeping me vulnerable. My oldest and closest friend. The person who knows me better than anyone.

'Please,' I beg, fighting back tears. 'He's just a child. None of this is anything to do with him.'

'Then you need to do everything exactly as I tell you, and no one will get hurt.'

With her arm still gripping mine, she reaches to the bedside table and opens the top drawer, pulling out a writing pad and a pen. She hands them to me.

'Your suicide note,' she tells me calmly. 'Write it.'

THIRTY-SIX
SUNDAY

'Sit down,' she says, pointing at the floor and talking to me as though I'm a disobedient dog. And I follow her instructions like a coward, weakened by the threat she's holding over my son. She stands over me with the syringe still in her hand, and she drops the pad and paper on the carpet next to me.

'To Noah,' she says. She glances at the window and then looks at me impatiently. 'Well, come on then... write it.'

I look at her through glassy eyes, unable to conceal my fear. 'Do you really think you're going to get away with killing me and trying to make it look like a suicide? The police are already on to you now... it's just a matter of time.'

She drops beside me, to her knees. 'Kill you?' she repeats incredulously. 'I'm not going to kill you, Suzanna. I could never hurt you. I'm trying to save you. I've always been the only person who could save you.'

Her words turn the blood in my veins to ice. I open my mouth to speak, but I don't get a chance to. My phone ringing in my pocket pierces the silence. Jonathan.

I take it from my pocket, and Jess snatches it from my hand.

She flings it across the room, where it drops down the side of the wardrobe.

'You're trying to take me away from my child. You've framed my husband. Who do you think you're saving me from?' *The only person I need saving from is you*, I think, but I don't say it. I've no idea of just how volatile Jess might really be. I've clearly never known her at all. Neither has Matthew.

I see Reka at the bottom of the staircase, as I'd seen her in a memory that I wasn't sure was real. I'd believed it possible that I had ended her life. Yet now, the distorted recollection of it fades, and the vision of me at the head of those stairs is replaced with Jess.

'Yourself, Suzanna. I know you better than anyone. When I first met you, I saw something instantly that Matthew never saw. You were broken even then, before Annabelle... before everything else. And you saw something in me too, didn't you? That's why we became friends... the best of friends. That's why you've trusted me with your therapy. You've trusted me with your secrets. You knew I was the only person who could save you from yourself.'

I try not to flinch at her words, not wanting to provoke a reaction. The longer I keep her talking, the more time I can buy myself to try to work out how I'm going to get Noah away from her. Jonathan will be here soon... perhaps the police. And she's not going to take me away from my son.

'Start writing,' she says, jabbing a finger at the paper. 'Dear Noah, I want you to know that I love you and that I'm sorry.'

'What are we going to do?' I ask her. 'You've obviously planned for this, and you know that I trust you, but I can't cope with things being sprung on me, you know that.'

For the moment, pretending we're on the same side and that I still trust her enough to want to hear her plans for me seems to work. She relaxes as she crouches beside me, though I'm still wary of the syringe that now hangs loosely in her grip. And I don't believe for a moment that she's convinced by my performance.

'You're going to disappear for a while. I've got everything packed and ready for you – fake passport, cash, everything you need. But the police need to think you're dead... it's the only way it'll work. I'm going to give you instructions. If you follow exactly what I tell you, no one will come looking for you. I thought we'd have more time, so there are things you're going to have to do for yourself. Everything's in the bag.'

I look where she gestures, seeing the overnight bag that's resting on the floor beneath the window. I realise now just how premeditated this has all been. Jess was always planning to separate me from Noah. From my family.

'Write it,' she says again, her words so flat and cold that I don't hear her voice at all. She turns to the bed and lifts Noah's limp arm, holding the syringe against his skin.

'Stop!' I cry. 'Please. I'll do it. Whatever you say... I'll do it. Please don't hurt him.'

I write the words 'Dear Noah', deliberately taking my time, the pen shaking uncontrollably in my hand.

'Why are you doing this?'

But she doesn't get a chance to answer. There's a hammering on the door from downstairs. At the other side of the room, where Jess flung my phone, it starts to ring again.

We realise it together: we've both run out of time.

'Everything has been for you, Suzanna,' she says, and her words are so convincing that I'm certain she must believe it.

She pulls her arm back before driving the syringe into my neck, and then the room begins to blur before fading to black.

THIRTY-SEVEN

SUNDAY

The first thing I see when I open my eyes is Matthew. He's sitting by the side of the bed, my hand held in his, his face turned away, head lowered, lost in his thoughts. I try to open my mouth to say something, but my lips are so dry that I find it difficult to part them. The sounds and smell of a hospital ward surround me: the rhythmic bleeping of a machine in another room, the unmistakable scent of hospital-grade cottage pie lingering from the corridor. I try to move on to my side, thinking I'll be able to shift my weight on to my left shoulder, but my body feels as though it's made of concrete.

Then I look at my hand... empty. Matthew isn't here; he's just a figment of my imagination. With a jolt of realisation that hits me like a brick, I remember that he's still in custody. And then I realise that neither of us is with Noah. Noah was with Jess. I have no idea where either of them is, or if he's still with her.

I push myself up in bed, feeling sick with the effort of it. I'm still wearing Jess's pyjamas, the ones I was wearing at her house, though I've no idea how long I've been here or what time of day it is. From the corridor, I hear voices talking near the ajar ward door. I use all my effort to force myself up, swinging my legs over the side of the bed and nearly losing my balance.

'Mrs Cross... you're awake.'

In the doorway stands a female uniformed officer. She moves back into the corridor, glancing up and down, presumably searching for a member of the medical staff.

'I need to get out of here,' I tell her. 'My son—'

'Noah is safe,' she assures me. 'He's being looked after.'

'Looked after by who?' I say, realising I don't have any shoes to put on.

'I don't think—' she starts, but her response is cut short as she lunges forward to grab me. The room spins as I lose my balance.

'Please,' I beg the officer as she helps me upright. 'I need to go to my son. He'll be terrified... please let me be with him.'

'We need to get you checked over before—'

'Are you a mother?' I ask her, registering the silver band on her wedding finger.

She nods.

'I'm fine,' I tell her. 'Just dizzy, that's all. Please... take me to my son.'

'He's in the children's unit,' she tells me, her face softening. 'I'll take you to him.'

She holds me by the arm like someone assisting a frail elderly lady, and she leads me into the corridor. When we pass the nurses' station, she asks for a wheelchair. We wait until one of the porters arrives, and then she pushes me towards the main corridor, where we take a lift to the third floor.

The officer talks to a member of staff at the intercom to the children's unit, and we're buzzed through into a corridor where the walls are adorned with children's drawings and advice posters on the symptoms of common and less common childhood illnesses. At some point, I'm going to have to explain to Noah how he came to be in the hospital. He may ask what happened to 'Auntie Jess', and I'll need to offer him honest answers to his questions. But for now, all I want to do is see him, because until he's in front of me and I'm able to touch him, I can't bring myself to believe that he is truly safe and well.

The officer whose name I still don't know pushes me along the corridor until we reach room 4. There's a teddy bear on the bedside table – one I don't recognise and presume has been loaned from somewhere in the hospital; all Noah's belongings are still at home, where they were left last week. Curled beneath a thin hospital blanket, with his back to the doorway, is Noah, looking even tinier than he did when I last saw him, a small bundle lying inert and unconscious on Jess's bed.

I get up from the wheelchair and go around to the far side of the bed, dropping into the chair that waits to be used by someone who loves him. His face looks so pale, but his eyes are rimmed with grey, this tiny person carrying a weight of woes no child his age should be forced to endure.

'He's just sleeping now,' a voice says, and when I look up, there's a nurse standing next to the officer. 'He was awake earlier... he's had something to eat.'

'He's going to be okay?'

The nurse nods.

'Do you know what he was given yet?'

'Too early to say. When the toxicology report comes back, we'll know more, but I promise you, you don't need to worry. There'll be no lasting effects.'

Only the psychological ones, I think... as if there weren't enough of those already.

'He'll do even better now you're here with him,' the nurse adds. 'He was asking for you.'

'Was he?' I see both women register my surprise at the fact. 'He barely speaks,' I explain.

'He'll be relieved to see you when he wakes up,' the nurse

says. She gestures to the buzzer by his bedside. 'Give me a call if you need anything.'

She leaves the room, and the officer who brought me here goes out to wait in the corridor, affording Noah and me some privacy. I take his little cold hand in mine, marvelling at how small and yet how strong he is. I make a vow to never leave his side again, and then the uncertainty of my future crashes upon me, reminding me that I can't make any promise that I might not be able to keep.

'I am so sorry,' I say softly, hoping that even in sleep, he may somehow be able to hear my words. 'For everything. I let you down. I let Annabelle down. But I'm going to get better, and I'm going to do everything I can to make it up to you, okay?'

I study his little face: the soft curve of his bottom lip, the dark lashes, the eyes that carry so much pain. I wonder if his sister might have grown to resemble him. I wonder if, in years to come, he will have any memory of her. Perhaps he'll have no memory of this, of Jess or Reka or anything that's happened this past week, and yet if not, the scars of it are likely to remain, a permanent reminder of a chapter in a life barely yet begun.

I may not be able to be there for him as he tries to heal, so all I can do now is make sure Matthew is.

THIRTY-EIGHT

SUNDAY

DC Western arrives at the hospital after Noah and I have eaten lunch together in the children's unit. I agree to leave him once she's promised me that a uniformed officer will be staying outside his room, though I'm still reluctant even then. Once I'm reassured that he's safe, I leave the hospital with the detective.

As she drives away from the hospital car park, she fills in the details of what happened in the time between Jess injecting me and me waking up at the hospital.

'Your solicitor had already called 999 by the time he reached the house. The police broke the door. Jess tried to escape. She was picked up about half a mile from the house. She had a bag with a fake passport, money, some clothes.'

'It was meant for me.'

Her left eyebrow raises.

'She told me her plan while she tried to get me to write a suicide note to Noah. She said it was the only way it would work, if everyone else thought I was dead. She's in custody now then?'

She nods. 'The search of her house is ongoing, but there's already been large amounts of medication found in her office.

Propofol, which we suspect might have been in the syringe she used on you.'

'What is that?'

'An anaesthetic used in hospitals. It takes effect quickly, as you found out. You're lucky Jonathan responded as he did... if he'd not called emergency services so soon, the outcome might have been very different.'

'What else have they found?' I ask. 'At Jess's.'

'The search is ongoing, so I can't say much more at the moment.'

'Will I be able to see Matthew, when we get to the station?'

'You should be able to. But he'll remain in custody... there's still the fact of his DNA under Reka's fingernails.'

I flinch at the mention of it, convinced now that there must be another explanation for it. I won't believe any of this is over until we find it.

When we get to the station, she leads me through the reception area and shows me into an empty room before asking if I'd like a cup of tea. I accept the offer, even though I know it'll taste like dishwater. She leaves me alone for a few minutes, during which I try to work out what I'm going to say to Matthew. He might not have killed Reka, but he still lied. And I don't understand why.

When I hear the door, I expect to see DC Western returning with a cup of tea. Instead, Matthew enters the room. He looks grey and exhausted, somehow so much older than when I last saw him. The DC follows in behind him and gestures to the chair opposite me.

Matthew sits, and for a moment neither of us seems to know what to say.

'Why did you lie?' I finally ask, because until we've got past this, I don't see how we can even begin to process anything.

'I didn't want to lose you.'

It sounds so simple. So easy.

'And then you were arrested,' he adds, 'and I was terrified of losing Noah.'

'Jess told me you raped her.'

With just a few, awful words, Matthew looks crushed. I register the reaction on the face of DC Western, who stands near the door, giving us space and time to talk.

Matthew opens his mouth to say something, but I stop him.

'I know it's all lies.'

'What did she tell you happened? Please... I want to know everything.'

And so I share with him all the details she gave me, from the smashed window in the kitchen to the slice of lasagne he'd never touched. He listens to me without interrupting, his jaw clenched as I repeat her version of events. When I'm done, he waits for a moment, trying to absorb everything.

While I sit here hating myself for ever having doubted him.

Eventually, Matthew speaks. 'Everything you've just said to me is what happened,' he confirms, and I feel the breath leave my chest. 'But not to her.'

My heart stutters. 'I don't understand.'

'She called me just after I'd left the house on that Saturday evening,' he explains. 'She told me there'd been an attempted break-in.' He goes on to give a version of events much like Jess's: how he'd gone over to her house, she'd refused to call the police, he'd texted the event organisers to say there had been an emergency. 'I woke up in her bed the following morning and I couldn't remember what had happened. I was naked... my clothes were folded in a pile on her bedside table. She'd left a note saying she'd had to leave for an appointment, like everything was normal, like this was something we'd done before. I felt so sick, Suzanna. And then I had to go home to you and act like nothing had happened.' He reaches for my hand across the table. 'Everything she described was what she did to me, not what I did to her. I tried to talk to her about it after you'd been arrested, but she kept dismissing it. Then she told me how she knew I was prone sometimes to the same kind of lapses in memory that we both knew you'd experienced... like she was suggesting that was what had happened that evening, as though it was somehow normal.'

'Why didn't you tell the police if you suspected she'd done something to you?'

'Because while I wasn't sure what had happened, I didn't want you to know. I knew how awful it would look, and I couldn't put you through anything else. Things were already bad enough. I just didn't know what had happened. I didn't know what we'd done – my memories of the evening were a blur. One minute I'd be thinking Jess had done something to me... the next I'd convinced myself I must have been unfaithful. I didn't know what the hell to think of her or of me. And then Reka...' He stops and wipes his eyes with the back of his hand. I haven't seen Matthew cry since the day we buried Annabelle, and I'm sure the reason he's withheld his tears has been an attempt to protect me. 'I get it now, Suzanna. I understand how you believed that you'd been responsible for what happened to Reka.' He stops and swallows air as though he hasn't breathed for the last few minutes. 'Sometimes, my brain seems to shut down for a moment or two. I can be in the middle of doing something at work, or I can be trying to get Noah to play a game with me, and it's like I'm waking up in the middle of a sentence. It's only happened since Annabelle—'

But he cuts his sentence short, still unable to speak the words. We sit in silence for a moment, both of us blinded by tears.

'You could have told me,' I say.

Matthew shakes his head. 'You were dealing with enough. I'm supposed to look after you... you didn't need anything extra to worry about.'

He looks to DC Western. 'I told the police about it all after my arrest,' he tells me. 'By that point, my hand was forced – I had to tell them.'

'They must have spoken to Jess about it?'

'But we know how convincing a liar she is now, don't we? Who were they going to believe – a well-respected psychologist, or a man being held in custody for the murder of his child's nanny?'

'She told me that my blackouts were a trauma response,' I admit. 'And all this time, I believed her. And then that day, when she tried to suggest that you'd been tampering with my medication... I trusted her even then. I am so sorry, Matthew.'

He shakes his head and reaches across the table for my hand. 'No... you don't need to be sorry. I'm sorry. I was supposed to be the one who was holding things together.'

'I'm sorry I put that pressure on you.'

He looks up at me. 'This isn't your fault, Suzanna.'

'It is if I've made you feel that you're supposed to be the strong one all the time. You've been grieving too. My grief isn't bigger or more important than yours.'

'That kitchen window,' he says. 'She must have smashed it herself to set the whole thing up.' He squeezes my hand. 'I am so, so sorry. I should have seen what was going on... what she was doing to you. To us. After you were arrested, everything looked different. I couldn't think about Jess and what may or may not have happened. And I hated having to leave Noah with her, but I didn't have any other choice. Without Jess, Noah would have been handed over to children's services. I couldn't risk that happening.'

And though I still don't understand Jess's reasons for doing it, I see now how she managed to tear us apart. Divide and conquer. She made each of us suspicious of the other, manipulating our perceptions until any hope of trust was destroyed. She made us question our own actions so that neither of us believed we were even able to trust ourselves. She knew we would be dependent on her to take care of the most important part of both our lives: Noah.

'She was setting this all up,' I say. 'Gradually planting seeds of doubt in my mind. And I let her.'

'It isn't your fault.'

'But I believed her,' I insist. 'If even for a short time, I still believed her.'

'She made me believe you were capable of murder. How could I have thought that of you? I am so, so sorry, Suzanna.'

I close my eyes for a moment, my head pounding with the weight of everything. I think of Jess and me in the garden on the day she'd taken Noah to the park – how she'd stood there at the flower bed, listening to me talk about speaking to Reka. Jess must have known then that I'd been responsible for moving her body. Who else could it have been? Matthew had been unconscious in her bed until the following morning.

All my actions had played straight into her hands, making everything so much easier for her. It would have been so much harder for her to frame Matthew had I not done what I did.

'The DNA and the skin cells they found beneath Reka's nails...' I start.

'Jess must have managed to take a swab while I was out of it,' Matthew says, desperately directing his words at DC Western. 'It's possible, isn't it, with the right equipment?'

'The search of Jess's house is ongoing,' she tells us. 'Until it's complete, I'm afraid I can't say any more than that.'

'But there's a chance she might have used something, when Matthew was unconscious?' I say, trying to put the pieces of that night together. 'Then transferred the sample beneath Reka's fingernails?'

It sounds insane when spoken aloud, like a plotline from the kind of Netflix series Matthew and I used to watch before Noah was born. But it's not impossible. It would explain how Jess managed to frame Matthew.

When I look at my husband, he looks as sick as I feel.

'It's all so premeditated,' he mutters.

'The clothing,' I say, thinking out loud. 'That extra therapy session she offered me because she was apparently so concerned for my well-being. She needed to be at the house so she could remove Reka's things from her bedroom, didn't she? It was never about helping me... it was all about framing you.'

'What did I ever do to make her hate me so much?'

I let go of his hand. Jess's words come back to me, sounding different in their echo.

You're a good woman, Suzanna. A good person. Matthew doesn't deserve you. He never did.

You're the only person who's ever been consistent in my life.

'I don't think it was ever about you,' I tell him. 'I think this was all about me.'

THIRTY-NINE

MONDAY

A little over twenty-fours later, Jess is charged with Reka's murder. When I return to the police station with Noah, an officer looks after him while DC Western shows me to an interview room. Matthew is already there, dressed now in the clothes he must have been wearing on the day of his arrest. My heart lifts at the realisation that they are letting him go. I take the seat next to him, and he reaches for my hand.

'Has she made a confession?' I ask.

DC Western shakes her head. 'She's not going to make things that easy for us, I'm afraid. But the search of her home and her laptop has thrown up plenty enough evidence to prove her involvement.'

'What did you find?' Matthew asks.

'Large amounts of medication, including Rohypnol.'

'Isn't that known as a date rape drug?'

'Commonly, yes.'

I squeeze Matthew's hand. He can't bring himself to look at either me or the detective.

'Your allegation against Jessica,' DC Western says. 'We wish you'd come to us sooner.'

'So do I,' Matthew says bitterly.

'But there's still a strong and growing collection of evidence. Suzanna, we believe she may have been switching your antidepressants for other medications – Ritalin and Prednisone, to be specific. Both would have exacerbated your anxiety and your moods, as well as have affected your memory and contributed to the psychosis.'

'Psychosis?'

She pauses for a moment while her expression slips from its usual impassive appearance. 'Jessica diagnosed your psychosis months ago,' she tells me. 'It's all in the records she kept. Her documentation of your mental health is incredibly thorough, as might be expected of any good health practitioner. But unlike any good health practitioner, she obviously failed to share the information of your condition with other relevant professionals.'

I look to Matthew. 'But she never said anything to me. Or to you?'

He shakes his head.

'She kept me unwell,' I say, my voice breaking on the words. 'She could have got me the help I needed, but she chose not to. Why would she do that?'

'To keep you vulnerable,' Matthew says between gritted teeth. 'To maintain some kind of control over you. She needed you to need her. I should have seen what was going on.'

'But poor Reka did,' I say quietly.

'We're still very early stages. But the texts from Ms Bako's number that were sent to Jessica along with the evidence the tech team has found have given us a good start in building a clear picture of what's been going on these past few months.'

'Tech team?'

'They've found orders for specific medical equipment. Kits that would have enabled the transferral of DNA, for one.'

I feel Matthew's fingers tighten around mine. 'Surely along

with the Rohypnol that would be enough to prove what she did to me that night?'

'We need some DNA evidence, really. There are test results still to come back. We're confident we'll find something concrete.'

'Why did she do all this?' Matthew asks. 'She's a successful woman, she's got a good career, a lovely home. It just doesn't make sense. Why would she risk everything?'

'Her career might not be going as well as she may have made out to you both,' DC Western tells us. 'A complaint against her was made to BACP back in August last year.'

'What's BACP?' Matthew asks.

'The British Association of Counselling and Psychotherapy. It's a governing body for Jess's profession. A client accused her of emotional manipulation, and there was a subsequent investigation. Jess was due to appear at a hearing next month.'

'She never mentioned any of this,' I say. 'I had no idea.'

'What sort of emotional manipulation?' asks Matthew.

'The client claimed that Jess exploited her vulnerability to make her increasingly dependent on her. Her initial email accused Jess of prolonging her therapy and using methods that had knowingly worsened her anxiety. When the client suggested ending her therapy sessions, Jess apparently became aggressive towards her. There's a whole backlog of evidence to support the claim – one of the team is still trawling through it all.'

'Control,' Matthew says quietly. 'Just the same as with you.'

'In your case, Suzanna, we've got a growing catalogue of evidence to suggest that Jessica had developed an unhealthy obsession with you.'

I feel sick at the thought of the lengths Jess was prepared to reach to keep me within her control. Yet the fact that someone outside of our family has also experienced her manipulation gives me hope for when all this goes to trial.

'What evidence?'

'Photographs, mementos… items of clothing we think may belong to you. We'll be asking you to look through these items to confirm they're yours.'

DC Western's expression changes, and she reaches down for the bag she brought into the room with her. 'There is something else,' she says gently.

I feel a knot twist in my stomach. A part of me wants to see what's inside the bag. Another wants to remain in ignorance.

She pulls out an evidence bag, something held within clear plastic and labelled with a number. There's a physical reaction from Matthew before I realise what it is; beside me, his body tenses, and his grip on my fingers tightens once more.

Inside the plastic wrapping is a soft pink baby rattle. When DC Western turns the bag on the table towards us, I see the gold embroidered letters that adorn its handle.

Annabelle

Silence rests between us as I try to make sense of what we're looking at. I'd bought the rattle from a boutique baby shop in Maidstone when Annabelle was four months old. Jess had been with me that day; she'd met me for a coffee after a nearby appointment with a client. I chastise myself for not ever having noticed that the rattle was no longer in Annabelle's room, as though by neglecting the details, I have neglected the memory of her.

'It's our daughter's,' I say, fighting back tears. 'Why would Jess have taken this?'

DC Western looks me in the eye. 'We were hoping you might be able to tell us that.'

FORTY

THURSDAY

Noah is in his bedroom building a fortress with Duplo blocks. I sit with him for a while, talking to him without expecting a response. It will come, in time, but not yet. We've still got such a long way to go.

I leave him to continue his construction when I hear Matthew on the landing, leaving the bathroom. He still looks so tired. He told me he didn't sleep longer than an hour's stretch at a time while he was in custody, and I understood it: my sleep has been much the same for this past year now.

'The rattle,' he begins, because since leaving the police station, neither of us has been able to say what we're thinking, as though speaking our suspicions aloud will be the final crack that breaks us. 'It's all my fault.'

My eyes narrow. 'What do you mean? What's your fault?'

Matthew looks exhausted, and he's lost so much weight during his short time in custody that his face now looks gaunt.

He reaches for my arm and guides me into the bedroom, pushing the door closed so that Noah won't hear us.

'He woke up screaming. *She was there...* those were his words. I thought he'd had a nightmare... I started to wonder whether he might have seen you with Reka in the garden, through his bedroom window. I just tried to distract him. But what if he wasn't referring to that night at all? What if he was referring to something else? To someone else?'

His words come out in a rushed jumble, each one tripping over the next.

'What are you saying?' I feel cold sneak beneath my skin, chilling me to my core.

'I don't know,' he says desperately.

'Who do you think he meant? When he said "she"?'

His eyes meet mine before he drops to sit on the edge of the bed.

'Oh my God,' he says, putting his head in his hands. 'He tried to tell me. Noah tried to tell me.'

I can't say her name. My brain can't make it make sense, even though every part of me knows it does. Jess. She was there that day, a shadow in the background, as she'd been on so many other days before and since.

'What if he wasn't talking about Reka at all?'

I hang my head. I'll never forgive myself for what I did in hiding her body, regardless of the influence that Jess had put me under. No matter how great my fear of losing my son, what I did was unforgivable. The shame of it will follow me to my own grave.

I sit beside Matthew and reach for his hand. 'You couldn't have known what he was referring to.'

'He was talking about Jess. He was trying to tell me that Jess had been there with you in the house that day... the day that Annabelle died.' His fingers tighten around mine. 'I didn't listen to him. I didn't listen to what he was trying to tell me. I should have heard it.'

Is it true? Had Jess been there that day? I can barely remember the details of that morning or the early afternoon. All I recall is the *after*.

'You don't think she...' But I can't bring myself to speak the words.

'Divide and conquer,' Matthew says quietly. 'She made us question each other... made us doubt everything we thought we knew about our family. Noah included.'

'You can't blame yourself for this. I'm just as guilty for missing what he was trying to tell me. What about that lullaby? The one I used to sing to Annabelle?'

But I realise now that I never told Matthew about hearing Noah singing those lyrics in the park that day, or him telling me that it was Reka who had taught him the words. I think I understand it now. Had Noah lied through fear? What exactly had Jess told him? When I think back now, I realise that he had changed around her, though I'd thought at the time that Noah was just different around everyone. All those times she'd insisted on speaking with him alone, when Matthew and I had believed her to be trying to help him navigate the grief and guilt he wasn't in any way mature enough to understand – what had she been saying to him? I hear her now as though she's in the next room with him, drip-feeding him lies and poison. Making him believe that his sister's death was his fault. Perhaps telling him that if he ever told anyone that she'd been there that day, he'd be taken away from his parents.

Is that what happened?

My thoughts are interrupted by the doorbell. My first thought is that it's the police; no one else other than Jonathan has been to our door these past few days.

'I'll go,' Matthew says, standing from the bed.

I listen to him head downstairs and open the door, and when he doesn't return after a few moments, I go out on to the landing, silently treading the floorboards as I listen for conversation from the ground floor.

My heart stops at the sound of an accent just like Reka's.

The voices fall silent as I get halfway down the staircase,

where I stop and stare. In the doorway stand two women: one younger, one older. The first is blonde and beautiful, an almost mirror image of Reka. Matthew looks at me with an expression I know must reflect my own. We are looking at a ghost.

I already know these women from the photographs pinned to the corkboard in Reka's bedroom: her sister, Celina, and her mother, Petra. Their faces are both flushed with grief, their eyes red raw with tears. Celina is clutching a folded piece of paper in her hand.

I brace myself for an attack of some sort, knowing it is all I deserve. I know this mother's grief, yet at the same time, I am oblivious. One person's experience can never be shared by another.

'Petra,' I say, when neither woman speaks. 'Celina. I am so, so sorry.'

I see Reka's mother's face tighten, and at her side, Celina takes her hand. I fight to hold back the tears that pinch at my eyes.

'Will you come in?' Matthew says.

Celina steps into the house first and Petra follows tentatively. I see her focus fix itself to the bottom of the staircase, and she grips her younger daughter's hand so tightly that it must be hurting Celina.

'Come through to the living room.'

Celina hands me the sheet of paper as I gesture to the sofa. Neither of them sits.

'What's this?' I ask. I scan the letter, recognising Reka's looped handwriting from the shopping lists and to-do notes she would sometimes write at the kitchen table. I'm unable to decipher any of the words until I reach my name among the Hungarian.

'My mother received this the day before my sister died,' Celina explains. 'She texted her and tried to call, but she didn't get an answer. She left messages telling her to come home, that she didn't think it was safe for her in the UK any more.'

Matthew glances over my shoulder at the letter.

'My sister was an old soul, that's what our parents always used to say. She loved to write letters because she loved to receive them back. She used to moan at me all the time because I was useless at it. I'd always end up sending an email.'

She turns to her mother and speaks in Hungarian. 'My mother doesn't speak English,' she explains.

'You've seen the police?' I ask her, assuming that since their arrival to the UK, they've been told everything. Celina nods.

'What I did—'

'We know. We know what you did. And we know what that woman did to you.'

'It doesn't excuse what I did. I will never forgive myself. I don't expect you to either.'

Celina looks at the carpet before turning and speaking to her mother. Neither can bring themselves to look at me.

Celina takes another sheet of paper from her pocket. 'I tried to translate it as clearly as possible,' she says, handing it to me.

Matthew and I sit down to read the letter.

Dear Mama,

We only spoke a few days ago, but there are some things I can't talk to you about over the phone (and you know how much I love to write a letter). I told you last week that I was fine and that everything is well here, and that's mostly true. I know you had your reservations about me coming to the UK, and I understand why you were worried about me working with this family. But I believe now more than ever that I was sent here for a purpose. Like a calling, I suppose. This family needs help, and I think I might be able to give them that more than any of us anticipated.

Suzanna has a therapist. She's also a family friend. They refer to her as Noah's 'Auntie Jess' although I've never heard him call her this (and yes, he doesn't speak often, but he calls me by my name, and I don't think I've ever heard him do the same with Jess). There is something about this woman I don't trust. She is too close to this couple. I thought at first that maybe she and Matthew were having an affair of some kind, but as I quickly got to know the couple, I realised that was nonsense. Matthew is a good man. He loves his wife and his child. I can see how broken he is by his daughter's death, but he tries to hide it, trying to protect Suzanna.

Jess asks a lot of questions about Noah. She corners me whenever she is here, but always when Suzanna and Matthew aren't around to hear our conversations. She asks me whether Noah talks to me. She wants to know what he's said. Why? Why does she ask so many questions about this child who is nothing to do with her? I know Noah senses it. He is different around her. He seems to tense up, but no one else seems to notice it. Perhaps it's a case of overfamiliarity. I suppose sometimes we don't see the things that are right in front of us. And maybe sometimes we don't want to. But I think somehow that she was involved in the death of Noah's sister, Annabelle. I can't prove anything, and who would believe me, but there is something about her that just isn't right. The more I think about it, the more it makes sense. She might have been close to this family before the tragedy – I don't know, I wasn't here to see that.

Please don't worry about anything – as I say, things are mostly good here. I'll be home for a week in the summer and can't wait to see you all. Please can we all go swimming at the lake together? I've missed it so much. The weather here is miserable pretty much all the time, so this is my only request. Well… that and your chocolate cake, obviously!

Please give my love to Celina and Papa, as always. I love you, Mama. Speak to you soon.

Reka xx

Petra says something to her younger daughter as they both fight back tears. I flinch when Celina reaches out to me, still expecting an assault; instead, she takes my hand in hers and clings to it tightly.

'My mother says this woman took both your daughters. She deserves to face justice for what she's done to us all.'

I am startled by a movement in the hallway. We all turn to see Noah standing in the living room doorway, clutching Benji the beagle. He looks just as he did the day he came to the kitchen, having heard me speaking to the memory of Reka. That was the first time my hallucinations had ever been visual. Before that, I had only heard things that weren't real – never truly sure of what was fact or fiction. For a moment, I had seen her. I had thought her there with me. How heavily Jess must have medicated me that morning during the extra session she'd been so keen for us to have.

When Petra finally takes her eyes from him to look at me, her eyes are filled with tears. A silent communication passes between us, and I feel it in the words that aren't spoken – for the lives that have been lost, and for those that might yet be rescued.

FORTY-ONE

TWO MONTHS LATER

'Do you feel ready to talk about her yet? To talk about the effect that she's had on your life? We can take things at your own pace, when you're ready.'

I sit on my hands, with their chewed-down fingernails and dry, chapped knuckles. I'm ready to talk, but I don't know where to start. More than twenty years between us... a whole history to sift through.

'You loved her, didn't you? Is that why it's now so hard to talk about her?'

'She was my best friend. Of course I loved her.'

'Of course.'

'She betrayed me.'

'And that must hurt.'

My teeth clamp on the inside of my cheek until I taste the metallic tang of blood on my tongue.

'I trusted her with my life, and she took everything from me.'

'Tell me about your friendship before Matthew came into your lives.'

'It was good. Better than good. We found each other at uni, and from then on, we never needed anyone else. I was the first person she called on for everything. Whatever it was – work, boyfriends, her health – I was always the first person she confided in.'

'And that was a good feeling, to have her so dependent on you.'

'I understood her,' I say, ignoring the comment, because I know exactly what this woman's trying to do.

'Were you and Suzanna living together when she met Matthew?'

'Yes. We were both from different parts of London and we'd moved back there a couple of years earlier. I was establishing my practice and Suzanna had recently got a publishing contract. Things were going well for both of us.'

'Until she met Matthew?'

'He wasn't good enough for her.'

'Do you think anyone would have been good enough for her?'

I move my tongue around the lump that has formed in my bitten cheek.

'He took her away from you, Jess. Was that the problem?'

'He didn't understand her. No one could know her the way I did.'

She uncrosses her legs and glances to the door, where a prison guard stands at the other side of the glass window.

'When did you start to feel that you were losing control? When she moved out of your shared flat? When she said yes to his marriage proposal?'

My fingertips dig into the backs of my legs. 'She still needed me. She always needed me... that was the point. No one else could ever give her what we had.'

'Except they could, Jessica, couldn't they? Matthew gave her what she wanted. And as his and Suzanna's happiness grew, your own began to dwindle, isn't that the truth? Your relationship with your ex came to an end... your business started to struggle.'

I say nothing.

'Let's talk about the accusation that has been made against you.'

'It's all lies.'

'Suzanna was slipping away from you, wasn't she, Jess? She was married now, with a young son. She had a loving husband, they'd inherited a beautiful family home. And then there was baby Annabelle. A picture-perfect family.'

She knows this isn't how things were. Suzanna was struggling more than anyone realised; even more than she herself was aware. I diagnosed her psychosis in those first weeks after Annabelle was born, but telling anyone else about it would have been throwing her to the wolves. No one could save her from herself like I could.

'This client,' the therapist continues, 'she was a replacement, wasn't she? A temporary one, at least.'

I shake my head. 'That isn't true at all. I did my best for her. I do my best for all my clients.'

'I'm sure you believe that to be true.'

I know what she's trying to do. I've used these same techniques in my own sessions, but she won't achieve what I know she's hoping to.

'When did you stop needing her, Jess? This temporary replacement.' She glances at her notes on the table beside her. 'You parted ways with her last April, just weeks after Annabelle's death. Until that time, it seemed you'd been reluctant to let her end her sessions with you. Why was that? Did you no longer need her? Did she become disposable once you'd found a way to regain your control over Suzanna?'

'None of this is true,' I argue. 'You think you know what happened, but you know nothing.'

'I know you were at the Crosses' home on the day of Annabelle's death. Or am I wrong about that too?'

A buzzing noise begins to ring in my ears. She watches me, trying to gauge my reaction. But she'll find nothing on my face to hint at the truth. Only Noah and I know what happened that day, though I suspected at the time that he would grow to forget it, the memory of that afternoon fading to grey like a half-remembered childhood nightmare. That was why I'd needed those moments alone with him afterwards, to remind him what he'd done.

'Here's what I think,' she says, crossing her legs again. 'I think you drugged Suzanna that morning, as you'd done so many times before, and then returned that afternoon with a view to offering your "help". Instead, you found her asleep... unconscious while her toddler and baby were left to fend for themselves. What happened then, Jess? Had Annabelle already sustained her injury, or were you directly responsible for that?'

'I could never hurt a child.'

'You drugged a child.'

'I didn't kill him.'

'You could have killed him.'

The buzzing noise grows louder. She wants me to confess to being responsible for Annabelle's death, but she won't get a confession from me.

'I didn't hurt Annabelle.'

'You drugged her mother. You created the scenario in which it was possible for such an accident to occur. Do you not see yourself as guilty in that regard?'

Noah had already dropped her. There was nothing I could have done. An ambulance would have been useless... it was already too late.

'Annabelle's death offered you an opportunity. A way that you could use Suzanna's grief to try to claw back your control over her.'

My eyes narrow. 'This isn't therapy. This is manipulation.'

The woman's left eyebrow curves into an arch. 'Am I wrong?'

I won't say anything else. I won't speak another word: not to her, not to any of them.

'You had a hold over the whole family,' she says. 'You must have thought everything to be back on track. But then Reka Bako arrived in their lives. And she cared about Suzanna, didn't she? I mean, she really cared about her. Her letters to her mother were proof of that.'

She didn't care about Suzanna. She was jealous of our relationship, and she knew she would never be a part of the family in the way that I was. She interfered where no one wanted her.

'And she knew, didn't she? She saw what Matthew and Suzanna hadn't, and she realised what you'd been doing. She was suspicious of your persistent interest in Noah. She found out you'd been drugging Suzanna, and she confronted you about it. And to silence her, you killed her.'

This isn't therapy. It's an interrogation. This woman should care about the people she treats, but she doesn't care about me. And despite what she may believe, she will never understand. No one ever could. No one, perhaps, except one person. One day, when she looks back on everything that's happened and she's able to reflect with the benefit of hindsight, I believe that Suzanna will see things differently. I have loved her like no one else ever has, with the intensity of a lover, the loyalty of a sister, the unconditional devotion of a mother. I was ready to sacrifice my career and my life for her. Everything I have done, I did for her. And one day, I know she'll come to see it.

EPILOGUE

SIX MONTHS LATER

The house is silent. In the doorway at the end of the landing, I look at the empty room, stripped of all furniture and traces of her. The crying stopped months ago, and I haven't heard her since. I like to think it means something, but I'm not sure what.

A hand on my shoulder startles me. I'd forgotten Matthew was also upstairs.

'It still feels as though we're leaving her.'

He squeezes my shoulder gently. 'I know. But she isn't here. She'll be with us, wherever we end up.'

His hand drops to my side and finds mine. We both stand looking into the empty nursery, for what will be the last time.

For now, we're renting a place at the other side of Maidstone: a modest three-bedroom semi-detached on an estate where we're surrounded by people who didn't know who we were until details of Jess's trial went public. I braced myself for a backlash, but it didn't come. People avoid us, but we can live with that. At some point, we'll start to look for somewhere more permanent. Noah's start at school full time has been delayed, but we'd like him to start somewhere new after Christmas. The child psychologist he's been seeing since Jess's arrest seems to have made progress already, and despite all the reasons he has to be doubtful of others, Noah seems to trust him.

Jess's trial was a long one, and she was finally sentenced two weeks ago. She faced charges of murder, attempted murder, coercive control, administering a noxious substance and perverting the course of justice. She was found guilty on all counts, and she received a life sentence, with a minimum of twenty-five years before consideration of parole. Matthew and I didn't attend the sentencing. After months of having the details of our lives cross-examined and being forced to relive every harrowing event in the witness stand, we were both traumatised and exhausted. It no longer seemed to matter what punishment Jess faced, only that we would be allowed to move on from everything that had happened with whatever pieces of ourselves and our marriage we were left able to salvage.

I pleaded guilty to perverting the course of justice and preventing the lawful burial of Reka's body. My history of mental illness and the trauma of Annabelle's death were used as mitigating circumstances for the awful decision I made that night, and when the extent of Jess's drugging and manipulation was revealed, the fact that I remembered nothing of what I'd done was finally believed. I was given a two-year suspended sentence.

'Come on,' Matthew says, letting go of my hand. 'Let's go.'

He heads downstairs, but I find myself unable to move from here, not just yet. I see Reka as she'd been on the day we'd searched the house for Noah and found him curled in Annabelle's cot, and I understand now just how much she'd been trying to help me. For those last weeks, at least, she had known to a degree of what was going on. She had suspected something, and she had been brave enough to act on her doubts. She paid the price for that bravery with her life, and I keep lingering on the thought that it can't be left to stand for nothing.

Downstairs, Matthew is loading the last of the boxes into

the boot of the car. Most of our things have gone to charity shops and the tip, with a view to a completely fresh start.

'There's something I think we should do,' I tell him. 'And I'd like to ask Celina for her permission. Her help, too, if that's what she'd like.'

Matthew eyes me with caution. Reka's sister stayed in touch with me throughout Jess's trial, and I know he finds it as surprising as I did, that she would wish to maintain contact. I suppose she sees us as a last link to a life Reka had lived without her family being part of it. I can't claim to understand her motivations, but I am grateful for her forgiveness.

'What is it?'

'We should set up a trust... a charity in Reka's name. To help families of victims of unlawful killings through their trauma and grief.'

I see the scepticism in his eyes and can read what he's thinking. I've barely been able to manage my own grief, let alone help anyone else with theirs.

'It worked for you,' I remind him. 'After Annabelle. All that fundraising you did... it gave you an outlet.'

'I was trying to run away from it all, Suzanna.'

'I know. And that's why people need people. Other people with shared experiences. What do you think? Please say you'll consider it, at least.'

He agrees to think about it before getting into the car. I stand at the passenger door and take one last look at the house. Then I get in beside him, and as we pull out of the driveway, I don't look back.

Because sometimes, the only way to save yourself is to keep moving forward.

A LETTER FROM VICTORIA

Dear Reader,

I want to say a huge thank you for choosing to read *The Woman in Our Marriage*. If you did enjoy it, and you'd like to keep up to date with all my latest releases, just sign up at the following link. Your email address with never be shared and you can unsubscribe at any time.

www.bookouture.com/victoria-jenkins

The book started with an idea for a midway twist: a protagonist seeing and hearing a character who turns out not to have been present for most of the first half of the book. The idea of a non-verbal child standing in a doorway and asking his mother who she was talking to had quickly followed. While mapping out the whos, whats and whys of the story, I happened to see an anonymous online post by a woman whose baby had died after being dropped by an older sibling while the mother, exhausted by sleep-deprivation and post-natal depression, had fallen asleep. The post was gut-wrenching and heartbreaking to read, and this poor woman's sense of guilt was unimaginable.

I started to research post-natal psychosis, and was stunned at how severe it can be. I read and watched accounts of women who had believed their babies were dead, who had thought that their partners or other family members had been plotting to steal their child from them; women who thought they were being sent messages through their televisions. I think every parent can relate to feelings of exhaustion and running on 'autopilot', but the condition of post-natal psychosis can result in harrowing and often violent auditory and visual hallucinations that can leave loving mothers feeling that they may either harm themselves or their child.

The Woman in Our Marriage doesn't focus on Suzanna's post-natal psychosis, though references are made to it in the visions and thoughts she thinks about never having been able to share with anyone. The only person aware of her condition is Jess, who conceals her knowledge of Suzanna's desperate mental health struggles and manipulates them to serve her own needs. As a portrayal of a family wracked with grief, I hope the book does its characters and the sensitive subject matter justice.

I hope you loved *The Woman in Our Marriage*. If you did, I would be very grateful if you could write a review. I'd love to hear your thoughts, and they really do help in getting new readers to discover one of my books for the first time. I love hearing from my readers – you can get in touch through social media.

Thank you,

Victoria Jenkins

X x.com/vicwritescrime

instagram.com/vicwritescrime

ACKNOWLEDGEMENTS

Thank you to my editor, Laura Deacon, who was so enthusiastic about the idea for this story – I have loved working on this book with you. Thank you to all the staff at Bookouture who have contributed towards the production and marketing of the book, as well as the copy editors and proofreaders who helped in making it shiny. To my writer friends Casey Kelleher and Emma Tallon – thank you for always being on hand to discuss ideas and listen to my rambles. You are absolutely 'my people'.

As always, thank you to my husband, who always supports my writing dreams and might one day read this book (if he's ever able to pull himself away from listening to podcasts). Thank you to my children, who make me proud every day, and are just starting to realise that I do have a job.

A big thank you to Antonia Collett, who read the first half of this book before anyone else was allowed to see it and was the first person (but not the last) to highlight the issues with my problematic timeline. You now, finally, get to see how it ends! And to Melinda Stefan, with the beautiful accent, thank you for answering my questions about Hungary, for making the best cake I've ever tasted, and for inspiring Reka's voice.

PUBLISHING TEAM

Turning a manuscript into a book requires the efforts of many people. The publishing team at Bookouture would like to acknowledge everyone who contributed to this publication.

Audio
Alba Proko
Sinead O'Connor
Melissa Tran

Commercial
Lauren Morrissette
Hannah Richmond
Imogen Allport

Cover design
The Brewster Project

Data and analysis
Mark Alder
Mohamed Bussuri

Editorial
Laura Deacon
Imogen Allport

Printed in Dunstable, United Kingdom

66540330R00150